Penthouse Variations on

threeways

Penthouse Variations on

threeways

BY THE EDITORS OF
PENTHOUSE VARIATIONS

Published in the United States by Cleis Press, an imprint of Start Midnight, LLC, 101 Hudson Street, Thirty-seventh floor, Suite 3705, Jersey City, New Jersey 07302

Cover design: Scott Idleman/Blink
Cover photograph: iStock
Text design: Frank Wiedemann
First Edition.
10 9 8 7 6 5 4 3 2 1

Trade paper ISBN: 978-1-62778-198-5
E-book ISBN: 978-1-62778-199-2

Certain materials herein were previously published in *Penthouse Variations* magazine.

CONTENTS

Introduction

More is better—so say the readers of *Penthouse Variations* magazine. Out of the many letters we've received over the years, a favorite fantasy stands out: threesomes. Our readers' confessions run the gamut from lustful longings to the ecstatic realities of three-way sex. For these sensual adventurers, the ménage à trois offers the ultimate erotic experience, with more partners leading to more pleasure than they ever dreamed possible.

The narratives in *Penthouse Variations on Threeways* explore the many facets of thrilling threesomes, but they have one thing in common: an open-minded desire to share that leads to limitless bliss. The young couple in Sommer Marsden's "Threesome by the Book" decide to open their marriage and discover what they can learn from a sexy older woman who knows exactly what she wants:

She pushed my filleted dress back and swept down—somehow still elegant—to tug at my demi-cup bra and take one of my nipples into her mouth. What felt like an electric current ran beneath my skin, and I found myself pushing my hips forward as she sucked that tender nub of flesh. She took advantage of my state by cupping my mound through my panties.

My eyes shot to Chris, and I saw him leaning against the wall, his hand nonchalantly on his hard-on. He watched every move with avid eyes and a half smile on his handsome face.

In "Secret Fantasies," Alison Tyler reveals how a late-night confession can lead to a dream-come-true experience for a group of close friends:

"You know that secret fantasy you confessed to me the other night?" Marcus asked, pulling my arms open and taking my shirt off me.

Of course, I knew, but my cheeks flamed up at the memory. First, we'd shared a half bottle of red wine, and then we'd shared X-rated fantasies. Luckily, ours meshed. He wanted to experience a ménage à trois with me and another girl, and I wanted to invite my beautiful friend Carla to join us in the bedroom. From the beginning, we'd always had a flirtatious relationship, but even as I whispered my desires, I knew I'd never have the nerve to turn my fantasy into reality. But apparently Marcus had.

While in Kelly Mays's "A Bold Invitation," three singles have one hot hookup when they acknowledge their mutual attraction:

> When I came back to our table I had to laugh. Brendan and Tim were playing rock-paper-scissors. It appeared that Tim had won, because Brendan's head mockingly fell as if in crushing defeat.
>
> "Lose something?" I asked Brendan cheerily.
>
> "Uh, yeah," Brendan said. "Let me leave you two alone."
>
> "There's no need," I said, sitting down beside him and running my hand along his arm. "There's enough of me for both of you to share."
>
> The guys looked at me in amazement. Then their faces indicated an unspoken question, which I answered by smiling and nodding my head. I stood and told them my room number.
>
> "Meet me there in five minutes," I said. "Both of you."

Without a doubt, the erotic encounters in this collection prove that three is a magic number.

Barbara Pizio
Executive Editor, *Penthouse Variations*

Double Pleasure

Bonnie Gibson

My husband and I were sitting around late one night watching the Marilyn Monroe film-noir classic *Niagara* with our friend Brandon, when Robert said, "Let's go."

I was stretched out beside Rob on the couch, wearing an over-sized baseball jersey and nothing else. "Where?" I asked.

Rob stroked my back. "Niagara Falls," he answered. The television's light cast flickering shadows across his handsome face. "We've never been there, yet it's less than a day's drive from here."

"Great idea," said Brandon, sitting up in his easy chair.

My husband's fingers tugged playfully at the hem of my shirt, but I didn't care if Brandon got a peek at my bare ass. Calling him my best friend—and Rob's too—doesn't really tell the whole story. I've known Brandon for years; we even went out a couple of times. When he went off to college and met Rob, he saw at once that Rob and I would be perfect for each other. He introduced us, and one year later, he was the best man when Rob and I tied the knot. These days the three of us are closer than ever. Brandon is at our place all the time. At that point, we'd done just about everything together—everything, that is, except the one thing I'd dreamt about most: three-way sex.

I've long fantasized about a threesome with my husband and another man. Four strong hands on my body, two mouths on my most sensitive parts, two hard cocks demanding attention... The very thought stirs my innermost cravings and makes my cunt all slick with excitement. I told Rob about my fantasy years ago, but it was always merely pillow talk, a sexy chimera to spice up our love life. More recently I'd come to realize that if Rob and I ever pursued my dream for real, the person I'd want to join us in bed was Brandon. Physically, he and my husband are quite different. Rob is tall, lean and wiry, while Brandon is on the short side, and no one would accuse him of spending too much time at the gym. He's sort of a Ricky Gervais type—and like the British comedian, Brandon is quite charismatic. I find him eminently attractive, a sort of yin to Rob's yang. The two of them made my threesome fantasy absolutely perfect.

Once I knew it had to be Brandon who joined us, I felt a sharp desire to really do it. I was ready to share the most intense physical pleasures imaginable with both of the men in my life at the same time. We would push the boundaries of our lust past any limits we'd ever known.

That night, as the guys hatched the Niagara Falls trip, I decided that when we got there, I'd tell Rob about my desire to enlist Brandon's help in making my fantasy come true. If there was anyone my husband would be willing to share me with, it was Brandon. Of course I couldn't be certain he'd go for it, nor did I know how Brandon would react, assuming we got that far.

The next day, we went online and looked into hotels. We found an older place that reminded us of the Marilyn movie; it seemed to have a lot of character. Most of its rooms promised a partial view of the falls. Unfortunately, the place had only one room available on the dates we'd chosen.

"So what?" I said, seeing an opportunity. "It says the room's got two beds. Brandon, we're practically tripping over you around here all the time anyway. Let's book it for a couple of nights. It'll be fun."

The guys agreed, so two Saturdays later we piled into Rob's green convertible with the top down. We left in bright sunshine, but by the time we arrived in Niagara in the late afternoon, the sky was leaden. Just as we found our hotel, a huge thunderstorm hit. Hastily, Rob raised the car's top. Torrents of rain came down so thick, we could barely see out the windows.

"Correct me if I'm wrong, but isn't it July?" Brandon noted dryly.

We grabbed our suitcases and ran through the gale to the office.

"No point in going out in this weather," Rob said a few minutes later, as we stood before the rain-spattered window in our room. All we could see outside were other hotels partly obscured in the misty downpour, and heavy traffic on the road out front. People scurried along sidewalks and hunched beneath umbrellas that threatened to turn inside out in the wind.

"Forget the falls for today," I said. "You guys hungry? Let's order pizza."

And that's how we spent the first few hours of the evening—talking, eating, and flicking through the channels on TV, just as if we'd stayed at home. Something felt different, though, especially after I went into the bathroom and came out wearing a blue satin baby-doll nightgown. Rob looked at me and grinned. "You're sizzling tonight, honey," he said.

Brandon looked over, let out a low whistle and looked some more. His eyes took in the curves of my figure, which were barely concealed beneath the thin fabric. My large breasts filled out the front nicely, and my long legs were bare almost to my ass.

I walked to the bed, lay down with my chin in my hands and pretended to watch the TV. I could feel the guys looking me over, undressing me with their eyes. My breath quickened, and I wondered what they thought of my behavior. I had planned on talking with Rob first, but here I was, pushing things along fast.

A late-night, made-for-cable movie came on. Brandon stretched out on the other bed while Rob reclined beside me and began lightly massaging my legs. We watched the movie and cracked jokes, but the actors had plenty of sex appeal. A love scene started, and I confess it was pretty damn arousing. The guys fell silent; I did, too. The room seemed to be getting warmer.

I must have lost myself in the show for a few minutes, because suddenly I realized there were *four* hands, not two, sensuously rubbing my shoulders and the backs of my thighs. I didn't move. The movie faded out completely; my whole being focused on what was happening in the here and now. Two hands slid under my nightgown and squeezed the globes of my ass. Two more hands gently pulled my nightie up high. Inquisitive fingers traced the sides of my breasts. A rush of excitement liquefied my cunt. *This is it!* I thought. I hadn't even said anything to Rob—or to Brandon, for that matter. My heart was pounding in my chest.

I gathered myself and sat up to face them. Rob looked so turned on; I almost jumped him right then. I could see that he was waiting for a sign from me, just to be sure. He had arrived at the same conclusion I had regarding a way to make my threesome fantasy come true. Perhaps he'd even discussed it already with Brandon, and now they were making their move. I grinned and gave Rob a slight nod, letting him know that, yes, this was not only okay, it was exactly what I wanted. I turned my gaze to Brandon and saw that he was totally on board.

I whipped off my nightgown. Rob looked at my full breasts, my firm midriff and my trimmed pubic bush as if he'd never seen me nude before. The gleam of excitement in his eyes made my pulse race. Brandon, who really was seeing me nude for the first time, regarded my curvy body with frank appreciation. "Holy shit, you're a lucky man, Rob."

"Okay, now you guys," I prompted.

The moment they'd finished stripping, I had them sit back on the bed so I could take hold of both of their erections at once. Rob's cock never fails to impress me—it's long and beautifully sculpted, with a tapered head at the end. Brandon's hard-on was perhaps an inch shorter, but it was wider around, with a meaty crown and a nice heft. I couldn't wait to feel that stout shaft driving hard into me. First, I wanted to suck it, though. In fact, I wanted to suck both men imme-diately. Dropping down, I lowered my lips over Brandon's shaft while keeping my hand curled around Rob's cock. Brandon moaned softly and ran his hand through my hair, urging me on. I wasn't used to a penis of such impressive thickness in my mouth, so I was compelled to start off slowly. I soon grew acclimated to this girth, however, and found that I could gobble his fat prick recklessly. From the corner of my eye I saw Rob watching intently, his face flushed with passion.

After a minute I released Brandon and closed my lips around Rob's dick. I was infinitely familiar with every detail of his lovely penis, of course, but I had never before been watched while I sucked off my husband. Having an audience made the experience ten times more exciting. I began to switch back and forth between the guys, sucking and slurping on their cocks as though I were famished. Brandon was moaning loudly, and I tasted precome leaking from Rob's glans. My own enthusiasm was reaching epic proportions. My pussy was soaking wet and eager for action.

Rob gleaned my desire and knelt behind me while I kept sucking Brandon. The next instant, I felt Rob's fingers at the opening of my cunt. I gasped and let out a desperate moan against Brandon's dick. Rob rubbed the flat of his hand back and forth against my dripping folds, making me tremble. I felt him spread my labia, and I knew he was preparing to slide his cock into me. For a second he paused, and in that moment I saw myself through his eyes: my ass high in the air, my head lowered over his best friend's crotch, bobbing as I worked to siphon the cream from Brandon's root. The image made my sex clench with need. And then Rob entered me, driving in deep with his hands on my hips. I cried out at the exquisite sensation. He pulled partway out, paused, and rammed home again. Brandon's cock tasted so good in my mouth, and Rob's prick felt divine as it rocketed back and forth between my legs.

"I'm going to—I'm coming!" Brandon bellowed. A split second

later my mouth filled with semen as Brandon's rod squirted. I was still swallowing that salty cream when Rob grunted and gave in to his own climax.

"Give it to me," I cried out, rocking to and fro on my hands and knees before bringing my lips back to Brandon's dick. I would have liked that amazing moment to go on forever, but then my own climax rushed up from the depths and burst upon me, taking my breath away. I felt like the luckiest woman alive.

At last Rob sat back behind me, momentarily out of breath. Brandon's cock popped free of my mouth, still twitching faintly. For a long while, no one said a word, but as I regained my wits, I found I was hungry for more.

"You're still hard," I said to Brandon as I took his staff in my hand. Quick as a flash, I turned around and sat down backward on my friend's prick, feeling it slide deep into my sloppy sex.

Brandon grunted in surprise but happily accepted my lithe body in his lap. As I began rocking my hips, he reached around with his hands to cup my breasts. My gaze locked onto Rob, who was watching us with rapt attention.

"That's it," my husband said breathlessly. "Let me see you ride him hard."

Hearing him talk like that not only fanned the flames of my desire, but the guys', too. Brandon started bucking his hips into me and rolling my nipples between his fingers. His cock seemed to swell even larger inside me. It felt distinctly different than my husband's pole as I rode faster and faster, up and down its length. Rob came over and kissed me while stroking my thighs.

"Look," I said breathlessly to my husband. "See his fat dick going into me, spreading me?" I leaned back against Brandon's chest and parted my legs widely to give Rob a better view. He bent and looked closely, and then I felt his fingers down there, sliding around my clit. I started to bounce up and down again, fervently riding Brandon's pole. Almost immediately I was overcome by the double sensations of Brandon's cock inside me and Rob's fingers strumming my button. "Oh, I'm coming again!" I shouted. Brandon threw his arms around my gyrating body and kept me firmly atop his rod for the duration of my climax. At last his body went stiff, and he came, too, his seed mixing with Rob's inside my pussy.

Just as I was climbing off Brandon, we heard a shout from outside. I thought at first that maybe our antics had attracted attention, but when Rob peeked around the window curtain, we saw what all the fuss was about. Darkness had fallen and the nightly illumination of Niagara Falls, which we could now see off to the left, was underway. Colored spotlights turned the cascading water bright blue, red and yellow. It was a beautiful sight.

Normally I don't sleep well in hotels, but that night I slept deeply. Rob woke me early Sunday morning. He was wearing one of the hotel's white bathrobes and a pair of slippers. "Brandon's found a way to the roof," he said.

I rubbed my eyes in the darkness. "What?"

"Come on, you gotta see this."

He handed me a robe and slippers. I put them on and followed him down the deserted hall of the old hotel, then up a flight of stairs. At the top, a door was ajar. I stepped through onto the roof, bathed in the predawn light of a fine summer morning. Puddles here and there testified to the previous night's rain, but now the weather was clear and fresh. Brandon, wearing the old shorts and T-shirt he'd slept in, was sitting cross-legged and looking at the falls. They were easy to see from up there, and they were stunning.

"It should get even better in a second," Brandon said. "Watch."

Just then the sun emerged on the horizon, turning Niagara Falls a sparkling, fiery gold.

"Wow," I said. "Look at that!"

We sat in silence, watching the play of light on the falls as the sun rose higher. Down below, the street was still pretty deserted. If I moved back a little and lay down, I would be completely out of sight from below. I glanced at Rob, who was sitting to my left. He looked sexy in the warm morning light, with his hair disheveled and his face unshaven. I glanced at Brandon, who looked similarly irresistible. Ever since Rob had woken me, I'd been thinking about what had happened the night before. The memory had me feeling quite aroused.

The guys were looking at me. With rising passion I pulled the sash on my robe and let it fall open. "Come here," I said, holding out my hands to my companions. Rob grinned, dropped his robe and lay down beside me. The feel of his hard body against mine fanned the flames of my desire. We kissed passionately, and then I pushed him onto his back and got on top of him, facing his feet. Hurriedly, I slipped my robe off my shoulders and tossed it aside. Rob reached for my hips, and I slid back a little, until my sex was right above his mouth. His dick stood straight and proud in front of my face. I lowered my lips and swallowed it up, while Rob dipped his tongue into my cunt. I moaned happily against his cock and wiggled my hips, impatient to feel Rob's tongue on my clit.

Brandon took one look at our hot sixty-nine and immediately pulled off his shorts. He went around behind me, where Rob was twirling his tongue in my pussy. "Are you going to fuck me now, Brandon?" I said, turning to look at him over my shoulder. "Do it. Get down on your knees and shove your dick into me."

He saw the lust burning in my eyes and did exactly as I demanded. Rob's tongue was still plying my folds and tracing figure eights across my clit when I felt the head of Brandon's cock burrow between my labia. His hands went to my ass and he pushed forward, sliding completely in. I knew Rob had a crazy view of Brandon's cock entering my hole, right above his own tongue. I knew he was watching Brandon's balls bounce against my wet vulva with each thrust that followed. Rob's prick seemed to swell even more in my hand.

"Oh, that feels good," I exclaimed. I stretched my lips around Rob's shaft again and lowered my lips all the way to his balls. Brandon quickened his tempo a bit, pumping into me with rising zeal. I've always loved getting fucked from behind, but on this morning, with the addition of Rob's dick in my mouth and his tongue flicking my clit, the experience was beyond compare. I kept slurping on Rob's pole for as long as I could, but the incredible sensations racing through my body mounted exponentially until I lost all control. My body rocked back and forth; my pussy clenched around Brandon's cock as my juices dripped down onto Rob's face.

After a minute I regained my senses, but of course my companions weren't finished, and neither was I—far from it! I was desperate to experience both guys inside me at once, one in my cunt and one in my ass. I was practically beside myself with excitement as I told the guys what I wanted. Without waiting for their reactions, I climbed off of Rob, and he turned around. Then I straddled his hips, positioning his glans between my cunt lips. Before I sat down, Brandon took a moment to coat his fingers with my honey, which he then slathered onto my asshole. Then I lowered my body, and once Rob's tool was buried inside me, I leaned forward and prepared to feel Brandon's cock squeeze into my ass.

I took a deep breath of anticipation and looked down at my husband. Rob met my eyes with an expression of sheer excitement and passion. This was a new experience for him, too, and he was enjoying every single minute of it. He kissed and nuzzled my breasts and then took my nipples into his mouth. Behind me, Brandon eased forward against my ass, propelling the hefty crown of his prick through my sphincter. I gasped and held still, adjusting to the feeling. Brandon pushed farther into my backside, gradually filling me up until I was stuffed to the brim in both holes. Rob and I have anal sex fairly often, but this was way more intense. *A girl could get addicted to this*, I thought as my rear opening acclimated to Brandon's penis. He backed out partway, then thrust in again, and I grunted with deep satisfaction. Rob began flexing his hips, too, lifting his rod into my molten core. I could feel both cocks moving inside me, stretching me as they traveled up the separate channels within my body. I had no doubt the guys could feel each other, too, through the thin wall separating their pricks. They fell into a rhythm and began fucking me harder, jacking assertively into me.

"Keep going," I rasped. "Both of you...fucking me..." I couldn't finish the sentence, because a new barrage of climactic explosions ripped through me, robbing me of conscious thought. Fortunately, I was sandwiched so tightly between Rob and Brandon that I was not dislodged by my wild gyrations. Rob came almost immediately thereafter, filling my pussy with a deluge of semen. Brandon then cried out and pummeled my ass for a solid minute or more as the gush of his warm cream filled my back channel. When at last he pulled out, some of his seed dripped out of my anus and onto my husband's ball sac.

We spent the rest of the day touring Niagara Falls, but it was our threesome experiences that I will always remember best about that weekend. Nothing changed between Rob and Brandon and me after that, except that my threesome fantasy is now a regular, recurring reality—and I couldn't be happier.

Playing the Market

WILLIAM CLANCY

Tracey works at the café where I get my morning coffee, and we'd often flirt as she pulled espressos and frothed milk. Though I'd been immediately attracted to her, it took a full two months before I worked up the nerve to ask her out. I didn't think she'd be interested in me because I am hardly her type: almost a full decade older, I'm the kind of guy who puts on a suit every day and spends most weekends on the golf course. Tracey, on the other hand, is young and free-spirited, and though I didn't know what she did in her free time, I knew that the barista gig was to help her pay her way through art school.

She definitely looks the part of the bohemian art-school student. Her blonde hair is asymmetrically cut and always looks like she's just rolled out of bed, and her upper arms are covered in 1950s-style tattoos. I thought both of these things were hot, but not as hot as her body, which is curvy and voluptuous. I pictured burying my face in her deep cleavage to feel the softness of her breasts against my cheeks, and I could only imagine what it would be like to have her thighs wrapped around my waist as I stroked in and out of her hot, wet pussy. As a result of my fantasies, I would get a raging hard-on on those occasions when our fingers touched as she handed me my change, and I wondered if she also felt some sort of spark. I soon reached a point where my dick would start pulsing the second I walked through the coffee-shop door.

Finally, I worked up the nerve to ask her out. "Sure," she said breezily, as though she'd been expecting such an invitation, and my cock throbbed as I pictured her naked for about the hundredth time that week. As I stuck a tip in her jar, we made plans to meet at a bar later that night, and let me tell you, that was the longest day of my entire life. After leaving the office at five o'clock on the button, I rushed home to change out of my stockbroker uniform. I was so excited I got to the bar early, and I knocked back a couple of shots of whiskey as I waited for Tracey to arrive.

I was soon so relaxed that I didn't care that she was twenty minutes late, although I was surprised that she'd brought her friend Meg to what I had assumed was our first date. *Oh well*, I thought, resigning myself to having a fun, platonic night with two new female friends, and I urged my cock, which was as hard as usual, to calm down and do the same.

Meg was a cute redhead with a slim, athletic body and a more conservative look than her friend. However, she was just as flirty, which made me even more disappointed about the fact that I'd probably be going home alone. That notion got even more difficult to accept after both girls had a few cocktails in them, which made them touchy-feely, too—with me as well as each other.

At one point, Meg excused herself to use the restroom. I figured that Tracey would go with her because that's what girls do, but she stayed behind and continued talking to me. Before long, her hand was gently caressing my thigh, getting closer and closer to the outline of my rigid shaft. I began to wonder if Meg was coming back or if she'd been brought along in case Tracey needed an out. When Tracey leaned in and kissed me, I began praying for the latter.

Tracey's tongue pressed against my lips so I opened them. Her tongue continued to wrestle with mine as she wrapped her arms around my neck and I dropped my hands to her sexy ass. As I kneaded the supple globes through her tight miniskirt, she mashed her breasts against my chest.

Tracey was such a fantastic kisser that I nearly forgot there were people all around us, as well as a third member of our party. I remembered, though, when I felt a hand on my upper arm that I knew wasn't one of Tracey's. My eyes flew open, and I stepped away from Tracey with that guilty feeling of being caught in the act. It was Meg, of course, and as I watched her whisper something into her friend's ear, I felt the ghost of the blonde's luscious lips lingering on my own. Moreover, I could still taste the bubblegum tang of her lip gloss, and I relished the flavor as I tried hiding my disappointment at Meg's return. I was certain that she was telling her friend that she was sick, or tired, or both, and wanted to be taken home, and I prepared myself mentally for my night to be over.

What happened next is something most men only dream

about—or watch on the Internet. Instead of making their excuses and leaving, the two girls started kissing, right there in front of me! As I bore witness to their sexy pink tongues slipping in and out of each other's mouths, I became so certain I was seeing things that I glanced around to make sure I wasn't dreaming. A guy at the other end of the bar gave me an enthusiastic thumbs-up, so instead of checking into the nearest psychiatric ward, I counted my blessings and went back to watching the sultry girl-on-girl action unfolding before me.

However, I didn't just get to watch; I was invited to join in. Tracey reached for my hand, and then she turned away from Meg and resumed making out with me. This time I tasted grape, which I assumed was the flavor of the other girl's lip gloss. That assumption was confirmed when the cute ginger's lips replaced Tracey's, and she immediately thrust her tongue into my mouth. That's also when I learned that Meg's tongue was pierced, and the feeling of the metallic stud against my own tongue was both new and electrifying.

As Meg and I French kissed, I felt Tracey's hand making its way to my crotch. When she found the bulge in my jeans, she gave my rod a squeeze that sent my senses into overdrive. She stroked my shaft through my pants until my balls were aching with lust, and then she leaned in and whispered, "Do you want to take this party back to your place?"

We couldn't get there fast enough. Time slowed to a crawl as I sat in the backseat of a taxi, flanked by Meg and Tracey, and grinning like a Cheshire cat. The girls, on the other hand, seemed much calmer, as though they had done this before. But when we finally arrived at my apartment, they became as excited as I was to be somewhere more private and we headed straight to my bedroom, where they joined forces to strip me of my clothes.

I sat on the bed, idly stroking my rigid cock, as they then turned their attention to each other. First, Meg pulled off Tracey's sweater, revealing a lacy black bra that embraced the most magnificent breasts I had ever seen—that is, until I saw Meg's. When Tracey pulled off her friend's T-shirt, I did a double take at her high, firm C-cups, which were held up by nothing but gravity. Then my heart skipped a beat when Tracey lowered her head to that incredible rack and took a nipple between her lips. She sucked hungrily as she hurried to work open the fly of her friend's jeans.

Releasing Meg's nipple, Tracey nudged her pants down over her hips and then stood so her friend could do the same with her skirt. This was no easy task considering the blonde's generous curves, but she managed, and my dick twitched in my fist at the sight of her fleshy ass and totally clean-shaven pussy. Next to go was her bra, and I almost came when her abundant tits spilled forth. Looking from girl to girl, I realized that I truly had the best of both worlds: one was small and lithe, but feminine in all the right places, and the other was soft and voluptuous.

Now that they were both naked, I didn't know which one to turn to first. But even as I was contemplating my choice, it was made for me as the girls embraced. In seconds, they were on the floor in a sultry sixty-nine, and with no conscious effort on my part, my grip on my dick tightened. As I watched Meg and Tracey eat each other's pussies, I jerked myself off, and though my view was mostly obstructed by their asses and thighs, I caught glimpses of each girl's tongue darting over the other's sex to delve amongst moist pink folds. My breathing grew heavy as I pumped my shaft and the girls moaned into each other's cunts. There was no way I could keep my floodgates from bursting open, sending a white-hot geyser of cream into my cupped palm.

With my softening cock in my hand, I silently berated myself for coming before I'd gotten to experience a proper threesome. But as I reached for some tissues to clean myself off, the girls joined me on the bed, obviously not ready for the fun to end. Meg sat to my right and kissed me, and as I sucked the taste of Tracey's musk off her tongue, the sexy blonde moved to my left and lowered her head to my lap. Her hair tickled my thighs as she stuck out her tongue to lap up the semen that still streaked my shaft. My erection immediately returned, growing long and hard within seconds. As the redhead's kisses grew stronger, Tracey wrapped her fingers around my root and took my dick down her throat.

Her head began bobbing over my length as I cupped one of Meg's tits and rubbed my thumb over the tip until she moaned loudly. Tracey was also moaning as she dragged her lips up and down my pole, and the vibrations felt so incredible that I was soon gasping into her best friend's mouth. My hand moved to Meg's lap, and when she parted her thighs to allow me access to her pussy, I slipped a finger between her silky nether lips. She was pierced down there, too, and she groaned when I flicked the delicate hoop back and forth.

Meg moved entirely onto the mattress, pulling me up with her, as Tracey removed her mouth from my cock just long enough to straddle my legs. As Tracey resumed blowing me, Meg positioned herself above my face and eased downward until her ass and cunt were mere inches away from my lips. When she was close enough, I thrust my tongue up into her hot, wet flesh, first licking her lust-puffed outer labia before moving to her inner petals. I swiped up and down her slit a few times before zeroing in on her swollen clitoris and sucking it with the same fervor with which Tracey was sucking my dick.

Meg's juices poured into my mouth as Tracey swallowed another surge of my pre-ejaculate, and then she began massaging my sac. The way her hands worked my balls as her lips and tongue moved over my shaft kept me on edge.

Suddenly, Meg started quaking, so I grunted against her pussy, encouraging her to come. I stiffened my tongue and began thrusting it into her hole as she writhed on my face. Meg shivered and shook through her orgasm, and although I couldn't see her, I pictured the sexy redhead clasping her tits and pinching her nipples as she rode the waves of ecstasy. Tracey must have felt the quivers of excitement in my dick, because she removed her lips to say, "Just wait—you ain't seen nothing yet."

With that, Tracey sat up, threw a leg across my body and positioned herself so that her outer labia hugged my cockhead as its tip nudged her entryway. Reaching blindly upward, I found her breasts and squeezed them gently. Then she bore down on me with all her weight, lowering herself over my unyielding erection.

Her moist heat engulfed my shaft. I was so overwhelmed that I neglected my oral ministrations on Meg's pussy, but instead of demanding more attention, she slid off my face and repositioned herself by my feet. I couldn't figure out what she was doing, but when Tracey's asscheeks finally came to rest on my balls, I can honestly say that I didn't care. Tracey's cunt, totally enveloping my length, was so snug that I thought I might come before she even started moving.

However, I was able to maintain my cool because Tracey, seemingly in no rush, took things very slowly. She rose up on her haunches, dragging her sex over my cock at a leisurely rate while clenching her muscles around my shaft. When only my head remained lodged inside her, she lowered herself at the same unhurried speed, until I was completely buried again. Finally, she raised herself back up and then stopped. Now, with only the tip of my cock wedged in Tracey's hole, I experienced an unfamiliar sensation a few inches lower and realized it was Meg's pierced tongue playing over my balls.

At once, I understood why the other girl had moved down there. It also proved that the girls had done this before, because they immediately fell into sync, one lapping at the sensitive flesh of my sac whenever the other rose to the top of my prick. Whenever Tracey would start descending, Meg would move out of the way so that the other girl's cunt could swallow me completely. The rhythm changed periodically, and Meg would suck one of my balls into the warm cavern of her mouth while Tracey hovered over my knob. The sensations quickly became so intense that I knew it wouldn't be long before I blasted off.

However, Tracey came before I did. Even though my eyes were closed as I reveled in the sensation of having both a tongue and a pussy pleasuring me, I knew she was approaching her climax because her whole body started quaking. I opened my eyes and looked down at the girls and discovered that Meg had an arm wrapped around Tracey's body with one finger between her friend's labia, firmly pressed against her clitoris.

While Meg stroked Tracey's button, the other girl moaned and writhed above me. As her movements grew wilder, I was forced to grasp her hips to keep her pussy on my cock, and though she no longer had enough control to move up and down on her own accord, her constant spasms—as well as Meg's constant tonguing of my balls—

kept me sufficiently aroused. Then Tracey announced her release with a shriek as her cunt shut tightly around my shaft, just an inch below my crown.

Her warm juices poured down my prick, and from the sounds of slurping by the foot of the bed, I guessed that Meg was lapping them up as soon as they reached my sac. I was getting close to coming myself, but then Tracey slipped her pussy from my cockhead, leaving me disappointed—until Meg's lips replaced it. The steel ball of her tongue jewelry was now teasing the most sensitive part of my body, and my ass flew up off the mattress hard enough to jam my length all the way down her throat. She was prepared, and she sucked me as her friend moved to straddle me, with one knee on each side of my rib cage.

Meg's tongue swished over the underside of my shaft, leaving trails of tingles on my skin wherever her piercing skimmed over it. Then she released my prick and climbed onto it. As she eased her pussy down along my pole, I heard the unmistakable sounds of kissing from above me, so I craned my neck and saw that the girls were mouth to mouth. They had their hands at each other's tits as they kissed, stroking, squeezing and pinching their fleshy mounds until Meg moved one hand to Tracey's nether lips. Now she flicked her friend's clit with a finger as she rode me like a cowgirl, and I prepared myself for orgasm when my shaft swelled in her canal.

This time, we all came together. Tracey writhed against my chest as Meg's cunt clasped my cock, which pulsated with the volleys of cream shooting through my shaft. The room filled with our sighs, grunts and the heady scents of sex. We continued moving as one as we reached our climaxes, though the girls came for much longer than I did. They trembled and quaked above me as the last drops of my load oozed from my crown, until Meg finally removed her finger from her friend's throbbing button and pulled her pussy from my softening dick. Then they both collapsed to the bed on either side of me, and we all lay there gasping for a good long while.

That concludes the unlikely story of how a stuffy stockbroker like me ended up in bed with two hot young chicks. Since that night, I've seen Tracey a few more times, both at the coffeehouse and on a couple of casual dates. She's mentioned getting together with Meg again, but so far that hasn't happened. For now, the memories of that night are enough to keep me satisfied. I figure that if it happened once, another threesome isn't entirely out of the question; all I have to do is find a way to get Meg and Tracey in the same place and let nature take its course.

Sky-High Threeway

Joy Perkins

My friend Kristel came over from next door as I was packing for a weekend in the mountains with my boyfriend. Kristel thought she would help by raiding my closet and tossing all my sexy lingerie into my duffel bag.

"Kris, it's just three nights," I said, laughing. "I'm never going to wear all this."

She rolled her pretty blue eyes. "You're probably right. Where you're going, you won't need to wear anything at all." Toying with a strand of her blonde hair, Kristel added, "In fact, I wouldn't be surprised if you and Stuart knock that old shack off its stilts."

"It's called a fire lookout." I shot her a salacious grin. "Maybe Stu and I will find a nice bed of pine needles on the ground somewhere…"

Kristel, from whom I keep no secrets, knows I have an insatiable appetite for sex. It's always on my mind, and lucky for me, it's always on Stuart's mind, too. We can never get enough, and the more wild and adventurous we can be, the better. Considering that we hadn't seen each other in three weeks, I was looking forward to an especially decadent weekend of sexual indulgence. I felt a little jolt of anticipation deep in my cunt just thinking about it.

"Naughty girl," said Kristel, with an I-know-what-you're-thinking grin.

Stuart is a college professor who works for the forest service each summer. He was spending July and August in a fire lookout in the mountains. Most lookouts aren't in use anymore, but a few of the more remote ones, like Stu's, still operate seasonally as aids to forest fire detection. It's a quiet, lonely job for the hardy souls who man these stations. Even if Stu should spot smoke, the excitement would last only as long as it took him to triangulate the location and call it in to the authorities. Of course, I hoped the only smoke we encountered this weekend would be the metaphorical kind as Stu and I rekindled our passions.

Kristel knew the story of how I first discovered Stuart's "anything goes" attitude toward sex. It happened when I first met him and his friend Mark, last summer at a mountain campground. Remote and heavily wooded, the location was beautiful but more primitive than most campgrounds, with no showers, flush toilets or trailer hookups. Just pitch your tent by a picnic table and enjoy nature. I realize that's not everyone's idea of a good time, but I enjoy the challenge of roughing it in the great outdoors.

Stuart, Mark and I had the campground to ourselves most

of that week. On the second evening, they invited me over to their campfire, and I found myself attracted to both men, an attraction that only grew in the following days. Mark, a full-time forest ranger, was a big, handsome redhead whose affable nature and easy smile made him instantly appealing. Stuart was quieter and rougher around the edges; perhaps that's why he especially excited me. I found his keen sense of the wilderness intriguing, and I was totally turned on by his lean, hard body, mysterious dark eyes, collar-length brown hair and trim beard. Stu and Mark, in turn, were not immune to my physical assets. More than once I caught them eyeing my sexy figure, which I've honed and shaped with years of outdoor recreation. I wear a lot of denim short-shorts and clingy tank tops when I go camping, and I remember the guys glancing with admiration at my firm breasts, my athletic legs and my well-shaped, tight ass.

Soon the three of us were inseparable; we were hiking together, cooking together, even bathing in a picturesque mountain stream together. It was in that cool, knee-deep current that the rising storm of sexual desire we had all been feeling finally came to a head one afternoon. I had just finished rinsing soap from my body and was about to wash my hair when I felt a touch at my back. I straightened up and there was Stuart, a twinkle in his hungry eyes. Obeying my own yearning, I turned to face him, and he ran his hands slowly over my shoulders and breasts. There was another touch at my rear—Mark was tracing his fingertips over my thighs and ass. The personal space we'd formerly adhered to while bathing in the nude had disappeared. It felt so good to finally touch and be touched by these two gorgeous men as the sun and trees looked on. Silently, we moved closer, each knowing that we shared a common fantasy. I pressed my wet body against Stuart and sighed as his lips met mine. His calloused hands thoroughly massaged my tits and worked my nipples into stiff points. He lowered his head and sucked each nub, causing a delicious pressure in my breasts. Mark, who was still kneeling behind me, palmed my dripping cunt. I felt his thick but careful fingers open my smoothly shaved labia and slip inside, exploring my slick folds. My excitement tripled, and I couldn't help crying out as he touched my clit. Impulsively we all looked around, but we were alone.

Right next to my feet, a large rock protruded from the stream. I sat down on its warm surface and guided Stuart's cock into my mouth. He had a hefty dick, as rough and rugged as Stuart himself. Visibly pulsing veins ran along the length of the shaft. As I traced my tongue up and down that throbbing monster, I opened my thighs for Mark, who eagerly dipped his face between my legs. I squirmed with delight at the first touch of his tongue, which felt amazingly long and sinuous between my labia. The tip flicked in and out of my hole as Mark lapped up my juices. When he started sucking my clitoris a moment later, I twisted and thrashed so savagely that Stu's cock popped free of my lips. With one hand in Mark's hair and the other fondling Stu's pendulous balls, I tried to concentrate on my future boyfriend's manhood. Stuart gasped and began bucking back and forth into my mouth. I'm not sure which I loved more, the sublime touch of Mark's lips and tongue all over my sex, or the tactile plea-sure of Stu's heavy dick sliding rapidly across my tongue. When Stu finally tensed up, I cried out with anticipation, eager to receive his load. A split second later, he bellowed something unintelligible and filled my mouth with hot cream. I kept sucking and swallowing that salty potion until Stu was spent. Then, more excited than ever, I had my two lovers switch positions so I could suck on Mark's tool while Stu ate me.

Mark's cock, longer but not quite as thick as Stu's, was refined and as smooth as marble. A thatch of red pubic hair adorned its base. The taste of Stu's come was still on my tongue as I gobbled Mark's lovely dick. He moaned and twisted his fingers in my hair, watching as I slid my lips up and down his shaft. Between my legs, Stu was sucking on my clit like a man possessed. White-hot sparks gave way to an inferno of pleasure that spread through my body like a wildfire. A sudden climax rushed through me, taking my breath away. I don't know how long I thrust my cunt against Stuart's mouth, but when I finally regained control of myself, I resumed my oral attack on Mark's prick and brought him right to the edge in a matter of seconds. Gently holding my face in his hands, Mark bellowed and sent a stream of semen into my throat. I drank up his load greedily, letting them both watch as I licked my lips clean.

Then I hurried ashore, picked up my clothes and shouted to the guys, "Come on!" I headed down the short trail to camp without looking back. Stuart's tent was the closest and the biggest. Dropping my clothes on the ground, I unzipped the tent flap and crawled, naked, into the hazy blue space inside. They came in a moment later. No words were said as they lay down on either side of me. I yielded my body to four hands that caressed my breasts, my belly, my thighs, my sex. Stu lowered his mouth to one of my nipples and Mark took the other. Together they made my back arch as they nipped at my sensitive flesh. My groping hands found their erections, and I curled my fingers around them both. It was time to take these two magnificent men inside me, to fuck them in unison. I was desperate to feel the sticky-slick friction of their pricks as they stretched and filled my two holes.

Stu, thinking along the same lines, rolled onto his back and pulled me atop him. I positioned the head of his tool at my sopping cunt, flexed my hips and sank down to his root. I could feel every nuance of his fat pole as it burrowed into me. Mark came around in front of me so I could lubricate his dick with my saliva, and then he went around back and knelt behind me. I leaned forward over Stu's chest, giving Mark easy access to my rear hole, then waited with bated breath as Mark's hands steadied my hips. A moment later I felt his cock in the groove of my ass, and then the bulbous glans penetrated my tiny hole. I inhaled sharply, flooded with the intense pleasure of double penetration. As Mark's shaft slid home in my ass and Stu's dick settled deep in my pussy, the three of us quickly found a rhythm that had us bumping and grinding ferociously against one another. The tent filled rapidly with the spicy scent of sex. I gasped with delight as they pounded into me, their sweating bodies holding me firm between them. All around us, the silhouettes of tree branches played across the blue walls of the tent. I could hear the rustle of the leaves and the more distant sound of the gurgling stream.

Our pace quickened as the final climactic moment neared for each of us. Stuart gripped me with a new urgency, flattening my breasts against his chest, while at the same time, Mark arched his back and started pumping into my ass like there was no tomorrow. A few seconds later they came as one, filling the air with randy grunts and shouts as their pricks spat hot come into my cunt and ass. It was so electrifying that I found myself coming unglued. "Don't stop," I cried, "keep fucking me, keep fucking." My own climax overtook me then, and my words morphed into little bleats of primal bliss. We kept rocking into each other for a while longer, drawing out the pleasure for as long as possible.

The next day we all returned to town. Mark headed north the following week to accept a new post with the forest service, but Stu and I stayed together, and the two of us have fantasized about having another threesome ever since.

"I wish I could go with you to visit Stuart," Kristel suddenly piped up, interrupting my reverie. I looked at her with a start, remembering how the story of my threesome with Stu and Mark had made such an obvious impression on Kristel. She had made no secret of her excitement. Now, as our eyes locked, the truth was suddenly clear. Why hadn't I seen it before? My best friend was not just open to the idea of a threeway with Stu and me, she was downright eager for it. As for Stu, I knew that Kristel's softer, more voluptuous body would be an unexpected pleasure, an erotic flip side to my lean, athletic figure. My pussy muscles contracted again, and I felt a flush of arousal.

"Of course you can come," I blurted. "What a great idea!"

"You sure Stu won't mind?" Kristel asked.

"Are you kidding? He'll be thrilled. Double the fun," I added. Kristel reddened slightly, and I knew instantly that she was imagining the possibilities. I finished packing my bag, and we raced over to her place so she could do the same. The next morning we piled into my Jeep and began our long journey to Stuart's fire lookout in the mountains. The last ten miles were painfully slow as I negotiated a rough dirt road with steep switchbacks. Finally, as afternoon thunderclouds stacked up in the volatile sky, the lookout appeared through the trees. Built in the fifties, the thirty-five-foot-high, steel-frame tower was like an aging but stalwart sentinel. Metal stairs zigzagged through the middle of the tower up to the glass-walled, single-room cabin on top.

Stuart came down the stairs to meet us as we were getting our bags from the back of my Jeep. As I'd expected, my boyfriend was pleasantly surprised to see Kristel with me. He gave her a quick kiss on the cheek and shot me an inquiring glance. I just smiled and slipped into his arms, raising my face for a kiss. Stu's hunger mirrored my own as our lips came together.

After a minute he pointed to a small wooden structure near the base of the lookout tower. "That's the outhouse," he said, and Kristel and I groaned. Then we followed Stu up the stairs to his humble abode. A crack of thunder rumbled across the landscape as we stepped out onto the catwalk. Stu looked up at the darkening sky and said, "It's going to rain buckets before this day's over. But don't worry, these summer showers don't last long." From up there, I could see the orange disk of the sun above the tree line, its edges made fuzzy by the mist that was rolling in from the west. I noticed a plume of smoke to the east and anxiously pointed it out, but Stuart explained it was only a hunters' campfire. He led us inside the cabin, and my glance fell first on the small bed in the corner. There was also a well-used propane stove, a wooden table and chair, and a stack of radio equipment that Stu used to make his reports and talk with other lookouts in the vicinity. Cell phones didn't work out here.

As the first raindrops began to fall outside, Stu poured us coffee, kicked up with shots of whiskey, and we stood by the windows to watch the gathering squall. A tempest of another kind was gathering fast—a storm charged with sexual tension. Kristel excused herself to go down to the outhouse, and when she reemerged from the little structure, she looked up to see Stuart and me on the catwalk, making out. We knew she was watching, and that made us go at it with greater gusto. Our kissing became heavy petting as Stu's hands went under my shirt to my breasts and my own hands squeezed his ass. Kristel came up the stairs without a word, and when she reached the catwalk she went straight to us, her desire showing plainly in her face. We welcomed her into our embrace. Kristel and I lifted Stu's shirt over his head, exposing his hard chest and torso to a smattering of big raindrops. Kristel cooed with appreciation and ran her hands over my boyfriend's chest, then kissed his nipples and traced her tongue down to his washboard abs. Watching her, I felt my own lust shoot into the stratosphere. The rain began to fall more heavily as I unbuttoned Stu's pants and reached in to fondle his hardening cock. It was as stiff as a flagpole, and I pulled it out into the evening air so I could suck it. After a few feverish bobs, I heard Kristel sigh, and I glanced up to see that she had removed her shirt. The cups of her bra were pushed aside, and her gorgeous tits jutted free. I couldn't see her nipples because Stu was busy rubbing and sucking them with zealous dedication.

We were getting soaked out there on the catwalk, but I don't think any of us would have budged if not for the sudden flash of lightning and the thunderous report that followed an instant later. We hurried inside the cabin. Stu paused just long enough to close the door securely against the rising wind and rain before joining Kristel and me on the bed. We practically ripped each other's clothes off in our haste, and then our bodies slid together, bare skin everywhere. The feel of Kristel's feminine curves against me, from her ample breasts to her supple thighs, was new and exciting, while Stu's muscular frame was deliciously familiar. I took hold of his manhood and lowered my lips over the rigid shaft. Kristel joined me, sliding her tongue up, down and around the lower half of my boyfriend's cock. I had never shared his dick like this before, and I found it to be an incredible turn-on. Kristel's eyes, bright with lust, met mine for a moment, and I felt something exchanged in our look, something white-hot and carnal that made us both redouble our sucking and slurping actions on Stu's prick. The meaty glans touched the back of my throat, dripping Stu's tasty precome and stirring me up even further.

Kristel and I continued to wolfishly devour Stuart's heavy thick dick for a while, but I didn't want him to unleash his load too soon, so I got on my hands and knees and aimed my rear end at Stu. Without missing a beat, he positioned himself behind me and let Kristel guide his penis to my sopping slit. Looking over my shoulder, I watched my friend's rapturous expression as she observed Stu's fleshy organ sink deep into me. I don't think she had ever had such a scintillating ringside seat before. It was the most erotic moment of my life, but then it only got better as Stuart started fucking me hard, ramming into my cunt.

Rain lashed the dark windows furiously, matching the fury of my ardor as I closed my eyes and bucked back at Stu with all my might. When I opened my eyes, I found Kristel's pussy right in front of my face, the thick patch of blonde pubic hair glistening with the juices of her passion. She had moved around to the head of the bed in order to open her supple thighs for me. I looked up and saw her smoldering eyes and her pretty face wracked with need. I did what came naturally and started to snack on her succulent sex as if I'd been doing it forever. The taste of her luscious cunt turned me on even more, and I ate her with an abandon that soon had her gyrating wildly against my lips. Her large breasts flounced against her chest, and it wasn't long before she gasped and shouted, "Oh god, I'm coming!" as her velvety sex convulsed and gushed around my tongue.

Stu's thrusts into my cunt gained strength as he watched me bring Kristel to her thundering climax. He squeezed my asscheeks and pounded me from behind without mercy until an explosive orgasm blasted through me from the inside out. My face was still a mere inch from Kristel's pubic zone, so my cries of pleasure were lost in the slippery recesses of her vulva.

I was amazed at Stuart's superhuman ability to hold back from coming, but I knew he couldn't hold off much longer. He stretched out on his back, his slick-wet cock waving in the air, and I watched as Kristel mounted him, her luscious body settling atop his shaft. She leaned back on her hands and ground her hips against Stu's root, making him shudder. I couldn't resist hunching over and licking her exposed clit, and then his penis, too, as it slid in and out between Kristel's thickened labia. Stuart reached out and slipped a spit-slickened finger into my pussy, and then another into my ass. I gasped and moved to sit over his face. He shot his tongue up into my sopping folds and over my asshole, while in front of me, Kristel bounced up and down on his rod with ferocious energy. Stu kept tongue-fucking my sloppy cunt as he pressed his thumb into my anus, and suddenly I lost all control, undulating against his mouth and thumb with reckless abandon. Kristel reached for my heaving tits and squeezed my nipples between her fingers, prolonging my wild ride. Before it was over Kristel came, too, her whole body wrenching around on Stu's cock and her hair flying every which way.

Stu finally let go. I felt the telltale stiffening of his body and his rapid breath against my cunt, signs that meant the cream was quickly rising in his balls. Kristel and I both hopped off him and gathered at his pulsing cock to stroke and suck him to the point of no return.

Suddenly the semen spouted from Stu's prick like a geyser. Some of his load decorated our faces before Kristel and I gained control of that creamy fountain. After slurping up all that we could, I licked Kristel's face clean, and she returned the favor.

That's pretty much how the rest of the weekend went. It proved to be as wildly satisfying as I had originally hoped, with the added pleasure of Kristel's company making it a threesome for the ages. Several more weekends remained before Stu's assignment at the lookout ended, and you can easily guess how we spent them. Needless to say, Stuart's post wasn't so lonely anymore.

The Big Catch

Josh Williams

When my friend Tommy told me he'd decided to hire a guide for our next fly-fishing trip, I gave him a hearty slap on the back. "At last," I said. "Now maybe we'll actually catch something."

Tommy and I love to fish, even though we aren't very good at it. We've been casting lines on Oregon's rivers since the summer we graduated from high school, nearly five years ago. Tommy got lucky once and reeled in a huge steelhead, but he hasn't caught much since. Neither have I, unless you count the old can I hooked while fishing the Deschutes last year. So I was pretty excited to have an expert along for our next trip.

The morning dawned sunny and mild as we bumped along the river road in Tommy's truck. "The tackle shop should be just a few miles ahead," he said. "The guy's name is Sam. He's supposed to be their best."

"Cool." I pictured a grizzled old dude with a beard, someone who'd spent his whole life on the river.

We got to the shop a few minutes later and went inside. Standing behind the counter was the most striking young woman I'd ever seen. Her good looks weren't exactly conventional, although her sparkling blue eyes, sensual lips and creamy skin probably could have landed her a modeling contract. This was a girl who did things her own way; I knew that right off. Her blonde hair spilled down in dreadlocks from beneath her hat, and her left eyebrow was pierced with a small silver stud. She sized us up with those gorgeous eyes of hers and smiled. "You guys here for a guided trip?"

For a moment, Tommy and I were tongue-tied. My buddy was obviously as taken with her as I was. Finally, he said, "Uh, yeah, that's right." He introduced us and added, "We're looking for Sam."

She toyed with her dreads and said, "You found her." Grinning at the looks on our faces, she came out from behind the counter and shook our hands. To tell you the truth, I barely noticed her teasing grin at that point, because my gaze was pulled lower. Sam's shorts, well worn and faded, showed off miles of her beautiful legs. Farther up, the swells in her partly unbuttoned shirt indicated modest but shapely breasts. It was clear she wasn't wearing a bra, and I could see the outlines of her nipples beneath the fabric.

"You guys ready to hook some steelhead?" she asked.

Tommy nodded vigorously, and I managed to croak, "You bet!"

"Grab your gear and meet me out back." After one last appraising glance at us, she turned and walked out the rear door of the shop. I watched her ass, which was absolutely exquisite in those skimpy shorts. Then Tommy and I hurried out the front door to get our stuff.

"The *guy's* name is Sam?" I said, keeping my voice low. "*He's* supposed to be their best?"

"Look, I set it up on the Internet! I just assumed—"

"She can't be more than twenty-five."

"Just because *we're* about her age and can't fish worth shit doesn't mean *she* can't," Tommy noted.

"Well," I answered, "this little trip sure got a whole lot more interesting."

We went down to the river's edge, where Sam waited in a drift boat. Soon we were gliding along with the slow-moving current. Using both floating and sink-tip lines, we fished along several miles of the Umpqua River, never seeing another soul. Sam showed us how to use different knots and flies, and she helped us improve our casting skills. She'd practically grown up on the river, so she knew the most productive spots to try our luck. Sure enough, Tommy reeled in a hard-fighting fish before noon. A short while later, I hooked one, too. Sam caught way more than we did, though. She released most of her fish, but she still managed to fill her bucket.

I must confess, however, that fishing ceased being my main interest from the moment I met Sam. I knew it was the same with Tommy, who turned on the charm as soon as we got in the boat. Sam seemed to welcome our attention; in fact, she was doing as much of the flirting as we were. What I couldn't tell, though, was whether she preferred Tommy or me.

The day had grown warm when Sam finally steered the boat to shore. We disembarked, and I saw a truck through the trees.

"That's our ride back," Sam said, following my gaze. Then she looked at her bucket of fish and said, "I've got more than I can eat. You guys want to come back to my place for dinner?"

Naturally, we both said yes.

There was a real charge in the air as we packed everything up and stowed the boat in the bed of Sam's truck. The tension became even more exciting when Sam said, "I'm going for a quick swim before we leave." We watched as she peeled off her clothes and dove into the river. What a body she had—slender and fit, with perky breasts, a smooth butt, and a wisp of straw-colored pubic hair between her toned legs. Sam's creamy-white skin contrasted with the deep blue-black of the river and the multihued green of the foliage all around us.

Treading water, she called out, "You two coming in?"

Tommy and I raced each other to get our clothes off. I couldn't help noticing that he had a hard-on as big as mine, and I'm sure Sam noticed, too. Then we jumped in, and the three of us frolicked playfully in the bracing river.

As sexy as the situation was, it proved only a primer for what happened later, after dinner at Sam's cabin. For a few minutes we were all busy clearing the table and washing the dishes, but then the other two disappeared. From the open door of Sam's bedroom came the sound of laughter and squeaking bedsprings. *Well,* I thought with a sinking heart, *that's it. She's chosen Tommy.*

However, that was when everything changed for the better, with Sam calling out, "Josh, what are you doing out there? C'mon, play with us!"

I went to the bedroom and found Tommy and Sam kissing on the bed, both nude. A woodstove in the corner added its flickering light to the scene. Sam saw me, sat up and offered me a devilish grin. The lust in her eyes was playful yet intense; just meeting her gaze made my cock swell to full size. Her eyes dropped to the bulge in my pants. She crawled over and worked quickly to expose the object of her desire. In a moment, my pants and underwear were down at my ankles, and my cock bobbed free, long and stiff.

"Sit down," Sam directed me, patting the bed next to Tommy. My glance drifted to his groin. Unlike my pubic zone, which had never seen a razor, Tommy was completely shaved down there. His erection, shorter than mine but thicker, was ready for action. I saw him eyeing my dick, too. We exchanged a glance as I sat down. Like me, he was a little nervous about this new situation, but no less willing to see where it might lead.

Sam could now play with both our cocks at once, and she wasted no time doing just that. With a shaft in each hand, she stroked and caressed our erections with a featherlight touch. "I'm going to suck these beautiful dicks, and then I'm going to fuck them," she said, her tone as matter-of-fact as her words were salacious. She was pumping our pricks faster now as her ardor got the better of her. She tilted her face up to Tommy for a long, sensual kiss. Then I, too, got to feel her pillowy lips on mine and twirl my tongue with hers.

After a minute, she lowered her mouth over my swollen glans, and I almost forgot about Tommy sitting there next to me, watching. Sam's heavenly lips and tongue drew most of my attention as she bobbed up and down, slurping hungrily on my cock. Before long, she switched over to Tommy, and it was my turn to watch as, moaning softly, she engulfed his prick in her mouth. Her lips stretched into a wide *O* as she dipped lower and lower down my friend's stout pole. After a while, she returned to me, and so it went for the next several minutes as Sam happily switched back and forth between us. Her pretty lips were soon besmirched with saliva and precome—and then with a full load of semen as Tommy's cock erupted. "Oh yeah," he murmured as his head fell back and the tremors of release tightened every muscle in his body. Laughing softly, Sam licked Tommy's cream off her hand and lips, then turned and licked up the drops that had spattered onto my own cock.

Watching her satisfy her lewd appetite for come pushed me right to the edge. She finished me off by taking my cock into her mouth one more time. Her tongue curled around my glans, coaxing out my seed. "Oh fuck, that's good," I cried, jacking between her lips. "I'm—" My dick finished the sentence for me, spouting violently as Sam sat back. My cream speckled her dreadlocks, her face, her tits, every-thing—even Tommy's stomach.

I flopped back on the bed, content for the moment to watch what happened next. Sam climbed into Tommy's lap and turned around to ride his rejuvenated dick in reverse, facing me. The naughty girl wanted me to see everything—the unbridled lust in her face, her pretty breasts as they rose and fell, her taut belly, and most of all, Tommy's prick as it vanished between the cleaved petals of her cunt. She had to be incredibly wet down there to take his portly rod so quickly to the hilt. "Ooh," she sighed as she settled her ass against his ball sac. After a beat, she began to lift and lower herself on his stick, which emerged shiny and slick from her depths. Her face glowed with pleasure, and her tight body bouncing up and down on my friend's pole was easily the sexiest thing I had ever seen. Tommy reached around to palm her boobs, but otherwise he just let her ride him, which she did with zeal.

My glance drifted past Sam's shoulder to Tommy, whose eyes

met mine. His face flushed with excitement; his breath quickened and he flexed his hips, driving his cock up into Sam. The reality of the situation was hitting me, too—my first threesome. I was completely hard again, and desperate to join in.

Sam sensed this, because just then, in a voice breathless with urgency, she said, "Come here, Josh." With Tommy's shaft still inside her, she reached for my eager dick and lapped my rod all over until it was slick. "That's so you can fuck my other hole," she said. "I want to take you both at the same time." With that, she repositioned herself astride Tommy so she was facing forward. He lay back on the bed, and she leaned low over his chest, so that her tiny anus was revealed in the spread of her luscious asscheeks.

"Put him back in me, will you please?" Sam asked, looking over her shoulder at me. Tommy's cock, harder than ever, had been dislodged from Sam's cunt when she'd turned around. I'd never touched another man's penis before. *What the hell*, I thought to myself, and reached out to take hold of my buddy's shaft. It pulsed in my grasp. I aimed it between Sam's puffy pussy lips, planting the fat knob just right, then watched as Sam sank down to take it all inside with a passionate sigh.

"Now you," she said, reaching back to pull her cheeks open. Kneeling between Tommy's legs, I maneuvered in close and gently pushed my slippery cock into Sam's back hole. Her orifice admitted my crown willingly enough and sealed up tight around the circumference of my shaft as I slid in deep. "Ahh," Sam muttered, "that's incredible…" Her voice drifted off as she focused her whole being on the sensation of two cocks penetrating her. Then she began rocking to and fro between us with assurance, her dreadlocks flying about. As I watched my cock cram in and out of her delectable ass, I could see Tommy's dick beneath mine, pistoning in and out of her pussy. I could feel him in there, too, as his knob slid back and forth just below mine in its own channel. I'd never been part of a DP before and I don't think Tommy had either, but apparently we were hitting the right notes, because Sam was going crazy. She especially liked when Tommy reached for the fleshy globes of her ass and spread them for me, making my thrusts go even deeper. Sam came moments later with shrieks of joy that reverberated off the walls of her small bedroom. Tommy was the next to climax; his cock popped free of Sam's pussy at the last moment and his semen shot up against the underside of my balls. Some of it even went into my asscrack—I guess the way I was fucking Sam left me pretty open back there—and the shocking sensation, combined with the sexy spasms of Sam's sphincter, put me over the edge. I pulled out of her tight hole and squirted my load all over her fair behind.

A little while later, we all crammed into Sam's small shower, and that was pretty fun, too. Afterward, we climbed into Sam's bed with her between Tommy and me, and we all fell asleep to the crackling of the woodstove.

In the morning, Tommy and I made breakfast for Sam. The weather outside looked gray and drizzly, but she wanted to go back to the river, and whatever Sam wanted, we wanted, too. So we piled into her pickup—Tommy and I had left all our gear in the back—and Sam drove to one of her favorite spots. She parked the truck, and we hiked down through the overgrowth to a place on the riverbank where we were utterly alone. For a while, we cast our lines, as intermittent sprinkles fell softly from the clouds, but I knew that the three of us were all thinking about something else.

Sure enough, fishing soon gave way to a mutual desire for

carnal pleasures. It was Sam who gave the cue. A sudden shaft of sunlight through a hole in the overcast sky seemed to inspire her. Propping her fly rod against a tree, she sat down on the damp earth at the river's edge and began to undress. Watching her, I absently dropped my fishing rod, while the rod in my pants once again grew long and hard. Sam shed her clothes completely, baring her smooth, pale skin to the rustling river and the tangled green banks. She reclined on her elbows, completely unconcerned that the ground beneath her was damp or that the ends of her dreadlocks were sweeping up bits of leaves and twigs. Her expression when she turned to Tommy and me was so full of desire that we went to her immediately.

I knelt down between Sam's legs and dipped my face into her pussy. The honey-blonde pubes adorning her sex glistened with the wetness of her excitement. Tommy, meanwhile, dropped to his knees beside Sam's shoulders and busied himself with sucking and caressing her breasts. She rested one hand on Tommy's head and the other on mine as we happily tended to her pleasure. Spreading her plump pussy lips with my fingers, I explored her pink recesses with my tongue and lapped up her juices. She quivered all over when I closed my lips around her swollen clit. Gently but firmly, I sucked that sensitive little nub against my teeth, which made Sam squirm more stridently. She arched her back, feeding her nipples to Tommy's mouth as she sighed happily.

A few more sprinkles suddenly rained down on us, speckling Sam's skin with gleaming droplets that made her beautiful body more sexy than ever. She got on her hands and knees, unzipped Tommy's pants, and took his dick into her mouth. I continued to eat her pussy, but I was doing it from behind now, with the mud-smeared globes of her rump right there above my face. The night before I'd been balls-deep in that ass, pounding away until Sam had screamed with ecstasy. Now her tight little hole was begging for a piece of the action again. I ran my tongue from Sam's luscious pussy up along her perineum to her smaller hole and licked around the puckered opening, then headed south again. Sam yipped with delight, so I continued licking back and forth from one erogenous zone to the other until her ardor was stratospheric. She pushed the fleshy lips of her sex against my face, until a final shudder tightened her entire frame. With a fierce cry she came hard against my mouth, drenching my lips and chin with her pussy juice.

I sat back for a moment and glanced over at Tommy, whose thick cock was still sliding back and forth between Sam's lips. Rousing herself from her orgasmic swoon, she began blowing Tommy's cock with a vengeance. I stripped off my pants and boxers as fast as I could, then knelt behind Sam once more and slotted my cock in the groove of her pussy. The moment she felt my knob nudging her, she rocked back sharply, making my whole shaft plunge inside her eager hole. Moaning, she pitched forward—taking Tommy's shaft deep into her mouth—then swayed back against my groin again. In that fashion, Sam seesawed between Tommy and me for several minutes, rhythmically taking us at opposite ends as she raced toward another orgasm. I held firmly to her hips and jacked hard into her, lost in a pleasure so sublime that I didn't notice when Tommy decided to slide underneath Sam in a sixty-nine. Suddenly, I saw his face down there, right below her pussy and my jackhammering cock. She lowered her mouth to his manhood and slurped away wolfishly, while he stared up at the sight of my dick pistoning in and out of her cunt.

Then he did more than stare. He reached up and started playing with Sam's clit. Sam responded with a jolt of pleasure that tightened her pussy's grip on my cock. A moment later, I felt Tommy's fingers on *me*, touching my penis as it thrust into Sam's syrupy depths. Things were happening fast. It all felt so good that I just kept fucking Sam like a madman. Emboldened, Tommy stuck out his tongue and lapped at the juncture of Sam's slit and my cock. Sam quaked from head to toe; I was so shocked and aroused that I felt the cream rise in my balls. My buddy was downright eager now as he applied his mouth and fingers to Sam's pussy and my slamming spike, lathering up the whole flashpoint. I couldn't take any more, and said so, bellowing into the fragile quiet of our wild surroundings.

Pulling out of Sam at the last second, I squirted my semen all over her back and buttocks. It was an impressive geyser that went on for quite a while; I felt completely drained afterward. Sam came a moment later, pushed to her second zenith of the morning by the relentless strumming of Tommy's tongue against her clit. She dug her hands into the mud and shuddered mightily through her lengthy climax. She never stopped working on Tommy's stiff pole, though, and he erupted a short while later, the cream spouting from his cock like a fountain. Sam swallowed a lot of it, but a few blasts landed on her chest and neck. Laughing, the three of us jumped up and ran into the river to clean off in the bracing water.

Tommy and I left for home that afternoon with an offer from Sam to help us use our rods again, anytime. That's an offer we could never refuse.

Naked Spare

HEATHER CROSS

Strike! I watched distractedly as the ivory pins tumbled to the floor, and then were quickly swept away. The opposing team cheered because that gave them a substantial lead, and a victory would put the winner one step closer to the league championship. Normally, I would have cared more about the match, but I had other things on my mind—and from the look on my husband's face, I could tell that Bobby did, too.

It was our group's turn to bowl, and Trish, the leggy blonde beauty who had recently become a member of our team, took her spot at the top of the lane. She'd only been in town for a little while, and she had joined the league hoping to make some new friends. Bobby and I were hoping to make her feel *really* welcome later that night. My clit began pulsing wildly as she got into position, and I felt myself becoming aroused when she leaned over to release the ball and I got a perfect view of the upside down heart of her ass, which was looking oh-so-sexy in her tight jeans. I discreetly brushed my hand across my husband's lap and discovered that his dick was as hard as a rock, not that it surprised me. He'd been extolling Trish's attributes—such as her big green eyes and grapefruit-sized tits—ever since we'd first met her.

Crash! Once again, all ten pins fell to the floor, but in our favor this time. Trish jogged back to the plastic seats, her tits bouncing slightly under her team shirt, and gave me a high-five. My palm tingled where she slapped it, and my pussy tingled, too. Looking over at Bobby, I saw him giving her a congratulatory hug and his hand drifting down to graze one firm asscheek as they embraced.

I was afraid that he was moving too fast, so I silently prayed that this bold move wouldn't screw up our chances for our prospective ménage à trois. However, Trish didn't even flinch; she was either too caught up in the excitement of putting our team back within reach of the lead, or better yet, she really liked it. I had no time to linger on that thought because it was my turn, so I jumped up, retrieved my ball and added a few more points to our score. The rest of the match went smoothly, and we ended up winning and advancing to the next round.

Caught up in the excitement of our victory, Trish accepted an invitation to come back to our house for a drink, so we piled into our Prius and headed there directly. Once we were home, we toasted our success and discussed the highlights of the game, the main one being Trish's amazing strike. Talking about it obviously thrilled her. At the same time, I noticed that her nipples had grown hard against her shirt, and her hands wouldn't stay still. They flitted around like little birds, first landing on my upper arm and then on my husband's thigh, and while I don't think she realized she was doing it, Bobby and I saw it as opportunity. When she eventually squeezed his knee, he caught her fingers, raised them to his face and pressed them to his lips.

For a moment, she looked shocked, sitting stock-still and taking a deep breath. She was probably wondering what she should do, but her next thought appeared to be of me and how I was reacting to my husband's advances. To show her that not only did he have my blessing, but that I also wanted to fuck her, I smiled, reached for her other hand and threaded her fingers through mine. She was trembling, though whether from excitement or nervousness, I couldn't say. I leaned forward and gave her a kiss while Bobby took hold of her shoulders and began working them with his strong fingers.

After a moment's hesitation—and some gentle prodding on my part—Trish opened her gloss-slick lips so that I could slip my tongue between them. As I gently swabbed the inside of her mouth, my husband's hands moved around to her front to unbutton her polyester shirt. His fingers brushed over my breasts as he popped open her buttons, and then they went to work on my top, too. When both of our shirts were undone, I glanced down and caught sight of Trish's black demi-cup bra; then I closed my eyes, grasped the back of her head and pulled her closer for an even more passionate kiss. Now, when our breasts pressed together, I felt the points of her nipples, even through two layers of shiny satin.

I soon heard the unmistakable sound of a zipper being drawn and guessed that Bobby was releasing his erection. From previous experience, I knew he was sitting there, cock in hand, watching the girl-on-girl action unfold. My pussy pulsed at the mental image of his stiff member, and I hoped that Trish would be as impressed with it as

I was when I got my very first glimpse of it. Long and thick, the head would be swollen and throbbing, with a pearly drop of precome oozing from the slit in the tip. Then, with the knowledge that my husband was watching and stroking himself idly, I let my hand wander to Trish's tits, where I caressed her womanly curves until she shivered.

She gasped into my open mouth, just as I discovered the plastic clasp between her breasts and made quick work of her bra. Her soft, warm flesh spilled into my palms, and I massaged her gently until her back arched, her body in search of increased contact. More than happy to give it to her, I drew rings around her areolas and strummed the tips of her tits. Suddenly, her chest really began to heave, and I realized that Bobby had rejoined us, worked open her fly and slipped his hand into the waistband of her jeans.

Trish let loose with a plaintive sound that arose from deep in her throat to vibrate throughout me. My own pussy melted as I imagined my husband's fingers parting her sticky labia, delving between them and pressing against her hardened clit. Maybe he was even slipping them into her hole. If that were the case, I wanted to watch him pleasure her. I needed to see the explosive action firsthand, so I pulled away from our embrace to get a better view and give Bobby full access to her writhing body and to divest myself of the rest of my clothes.

Bobby tugged her shirt the rest of the way off as I helped her wriggle out of her jeans. She raised her ass so I could yank down her panties, which were rose-colored and soaked all the way through at the crotch. Underneath, I was excited to find a clean-shaven cunt, as though she'd somehow known that something extra special was going to happen that night. I, for one, planned on fully enjoying those silky, dew-coated lips, and I hoped she'd want to return the favor.

When I leaned forward, her labia peeled back on their own accord as if from the heat of my breath in such close proximity. Sticking out my tongue, I swiped it along the length of her slit, which tasted like salt and sugar. Her juices dripped down my chin as I lapped at her wolfishly, and I gulped them down as though they were nectar. From above me, I could hear her gasping, a sound that seemed to quicken the harder I ate her, but then it suddenly ceased. Forced to stop what I was doing and look up, I was treated to the beautiful sight of Trish with her cheeks bulging to capacity, her mouth full of my husband's big dick.

Bobby was kneeling next to her so her head was turned to the side, bobbing back and forth as she slid her mouth over him. Her lips formed a tight ring around his swollen shaft, which soon became shiny as she slid up and down his trunk-like length. I could almost taste the pre-ejaculatory fluids that undoubtedly flowed down her throat; they'd be as salty as the pussy juices drying on my now-idle lips. I licked them clean, trying to memorize her flavor, as well as the image of Bobby with his head thrown back while he enjoyed her oral ministrations.

He let out a loud groan, leading me to wonder what sorts of tricks she was doing with her tongue. Making a mental note to ask him later, I once again dipped my head between her widely splayed thighs, not stopping until my tongue bumped against her moist center. Her ass immediately rose up off the couch, her pelvis crashing against my face and enticing me to lick her even harder. I zeroed in on her clit with my tongue and felt it pulse at the heightened pressure. My own button throbbed in its desire to be touched, too, but unfortunately, my husband was too involved in the blow job he was receiving to come to my aid.

That left me no choice but to help myself, so I slipped a hand between my thighs and reached for my cunt. Now, as I continued laving Trish's pussy, I stroked my own slick petals until I was shivering as hard as she was. However, before I could bring myself—or my partner—to orgasm, my husband came to my rescue. Pulling my hand from my pussy, and his prick from Trish's mouth, he repositioned himself behind me.

I felt his cockhead nudge my nether lips as he grasped my hips, so I parted my thighs to give him better access. When the first inch slipped inside, I groaned and the sound was muffled by the folds of Trish's cunt. I sighed against her sex as the rest of his length quickly followed, stretching my canal. My muscles gripped him tightly as he rested inside me for a moment, then he pulled out until once again I was only filled with his bulbous crown. He immediately shoved all the way back in, my tits bouncing with the force of his thrust, and I felt his sac brush against my rear cheeks. I had to hold myself steady as it grew increasingly difficult to continue pleasuring our sexy third, but I did whatever I could with my lips, tongue and even teeth. I sucked and nipped her quivering sex while my husband stroked in and out of mine, and soon we were all grunting contentedly.

Then Bobby pulled me off Trish and flipped me over so that I was on my back and looking up at them both. Though Trish gave a surprised gasp, she barely missed a beat; she promptly climbed onto my face so I could resume sucking her cunt. My husband resumed fucking mine, and we became a mass of sweaty, heaving flesh, all of us racing closer to our inevitable peaks. I wanted Bobby to come in Trish's pussy, but I couldn't even suggest that with it plastered to my mouth. Besides, I was too late: a split second after I'd had that thought, his shaft pulsed in my cunt as he filled me with warm cream. I began to jerk as the viscous fluid splashed my insides and my teeth bumped against Trish's sensitive flesh, which set her off as well. A fresh flow of pussy juice poured down my throat, and I gulped it as I shivered and shook through a violent climax.

I was still moaning against my new friend's sex as Bobby ceased moving between my legs. Trish climbed off my face and slumped wearily against the cushions, still panting from her orgasm. We were all out of breath, and although my husband had pulled his dick out of my pussy, I still tingled down there. Curled up on a couch, I sighed contentedly, and Bobby gave my ass a playful smack before inviting Trish to spend the night.

Since it was late and her car was still parked in the bowling alley lot, she accepted. I was glad; I had a feeling that the fun was far from over, and I still hoped for an opportunity to watch my husband fucking her. The option of offering her the guest room wasn't even considered; we retired to the master bedroom where we all got into our California king, purchased with the express intention of sleeping—or not sleeping—three people comfortably.

As Bobby stretched out in the middle of the mattress, we girls flanked him on either side. I'd assumed that he or I would be the one to get the action started again, but to my great surprise, Trish reached for his flaccid cock without any prompting and stroked it back to life. I could tell that he really liked her because I had never seen him get that hard again so quickly, especially with someone new. Within seconds, his erection was standing tall and proud, and she was manipulating his balls with one hand while swooping her mouth down over his length.

I watched as her lips moved down and then back up his turgid shaft, and though I enjoyed the sight, I hoped that she wasn't going to suck him to completion. Although it would have been totally hot to see him filling the pretty blonde's mouth with his cream, I wanted to see his dick pumping away at her pussy even more. Eventually, my wish was granted; as soon as she'd gotten Bobby good and wet, Trish released him from her mouth and rose up to swing her leg across his pelvis. Then she grasped hold of him by the root and guided his member between sodden pussy lips that were still swollen from my oral attention.

Reaching up, he held on to her hips as she sank onto his pole. I watched as his shaft disappeared into her body until her ass rested on his upper thighs, then she raised herself back up until only the mushroom-shaped tip of his dick was trapped in her clasping hole. Her tits bounced as she repeated the entire process again and again, and as her pace increased, her breasts really started to jiggle. My cunt pulsed in sync with her rhythm, and so as not to be left out, I climbed onto my husband's face and lowered my sex to his mouth.

Now I could both watch the action and be part of it. As Trish rode my husband's penis, he stretched out his marvelous tongue and swiped it along my slit. The pressure building inside me rapidly increased as he laved my slippery flesh and sucked on my protruding clit. I figured that a similar pressure was growing inside Trish because her eyes were closed tight, her head was thrown back and although her mouth gaped wide open, no sound seemed to be coming out. If she were making any noise, I wouldn't have heard it over my own impassioned moans, which grew louder as Bobby ate me to ecstasy. Then Trish suddenly snapped to attention and looked me straight in the eye before leaning forward to press her lips against mine.

I forced my tongue into her mouth again, and she sucked it

hungrily this time, getting a taste of herself on my lips. Although Bobby was endeavoring to keep her steady with a firm grip on her hips, I saw that she was having some trouble balancing herself. Grabbing the back of her head, I held her more tightly against me so that she could continue bouncing on my husband's prick. Once again, our breasts mashed together, and I felt the rise and fall of her chest as she panted. I was huffing and puffing, too, as was Bobby, whose hot breath gusted against my damp labia.

Supporting herself against my body, Trish dropped her hands to my tits and held on for dear life as her ass repeatedly crashed onto Bobby's upper thighs. Getting ahold of herself, she manipulated my nipples between her thumbs and forefingers, pinching and twisting the rubbery nubs. Because the tips of my breasts are highly sensitive, I started to quake immediately, a feeling that originated in the pit of my stomach and quickly spread throughout my body. Soon, I was aquiver from limb to limb, and even the top of my head was tingling.

Mere seconds had passed before my knees shut tight against Bobby's ears and my cunt came crashing down onto his mouth. As my orgasm ripped through me, rendering me practically useless, I felt his tongue continue moving, but now it was inside me, having slithered its way into my seizing hole. When Trish realized that she'd caused this meltdown, she lowered her mouth and gave one breast a good laving while she attended to the other with feathery fingertips. However, in doing so, she'd inadvertently stopped moving her cunt over my husband's prick.

I realized this as soon as I'd reached the apex of my own pleasure, and since I was already satisfied, I moved away to allow my two partners to finish without me. That decision wasn't entirely selfless; I was excited to watch them come and create a video in my mind that I could access in the future. Knowing that this was my MO, Bobby quickly flipped the two of them over so that Trish was on her back with her legs raised high in the air as he knelt between her thighs with his dick still lodged deep in her cunt.

Grasping her by the ankles, he hooked them over his shoulders and began pumping away. The muscles in her thighs rippled as she held on tightly and enjoyed his steady strokes. I observed how my husband's asscheeks were clenched and how his sac swung back and forth. He buried his length in Trish's pussy and pulled it back out again and again, allowing me to once again delight in the sight of his hard flesh glistening with her copious fluids. Leaning in for a better view, I breathed in the heady scent of their combined passion, and when my husband slowed his pace slightly, I swiped some of her juice from his prick with my tongue. He grunted, so I did it again, relishing his flavor, but I guess the added stimulation was too much for Bobby because he started slamming into Trish so hard that I had to scurry to get out of the way.

That was fine; I could savor the taste of them on my lips while I watched them race to their finish. Trish's ass rose off the mattress as she bucked her hips to meet his inward thrusts, and her labia grasped his shaft every time he yanked it out. I admired how much her hole was stretched to accommodate his impressive girth and the sight of her quivering clitoris that was swollen large with arousal. I longed to wrap my lips around the protruding button to help her reach her peak, but then Bobby did the honors by reaching down and pressing against it with the ball of his calloused thumb.

Giving a loud yelp, Trish dug her ankles into my husband's

shoulders as her butt flew completely off the bed. His asscheeks clenched more tightly as he drove his cock into her pussy one more time and then froze completely. Now, the only movement in his entire body was a barely perceptible writhing of his hips and a slight quivering of his balls as he painted our lover from the inside with numerous blasts of cream. Her legs trembled as he filled her to the brim, and this time I was fairly certain it was from being so expertly pleasured. I also guessed that it was due to having her legs suspended on my husband's shoulders for such a long time, so as soon as I saw they were done, I helped her lower them back to the mattress, being as gentle as I possibly could.

Bobby withdrew his dick from her cunt, and we both watched as her hole closed, although a little fluid still managed to seep out. It dripped down one asscheek and onto the sheets. Looking up, my husband and I shared a loving smile before we both turned to our new friend/lover. When she smiled back at us warmly, the lids of her eyes heavy with satisfaction and fatigue, I felt certain that we had played a perfect game.

My Amorous Amazons

Joe Mason

My wife is a confident, powerful and beautiful woman. Back when we were dating, I often wondered how I'd gotten so lucky. Oh, I'd dated beautiful women before, and I'm not all that bad looking myself. There is, however, a physical difference between us that sometimes causes people to wonder what she's doing with me. Suzanne is a statuesque six feet tall, while I am about five-foot-seven if I stand up very straight. Add to this the fact that she always wears high heels, and you can understand why we often draw second glances from strangers. But neither of us cares the least bit what others think because we've developed a mutually satisfying, loving relationship that fulfills our deepest needs.

We recently celebrated our tenth wedding anniversary, and she gave me a better gift than I could have ever dreamed of receiving. The evening started out fairly low-key, with dinner at our favorite restaurant. Suzanne seemed particularly amorous all the way home. Once we got inside our front door, she showed me how hot she had become, pulling me close and kissing me long and hard.

Then she smiled and pulled a scarf from her pocket.

"Wait," she said softly. "I have a surprise for you tonight. Let's go to the room."

She blindfolded me with the scarf and led me into our special room, a spare bedroom we had outfitted with a variety of accoutrements to enhance our sexual play. I heard her strike a match and caught a whiff of scented candles. Then there was a rustle of clothing that sounded like she was removing her dress. I soon knew I had guessed correctly as she kissed me lightly on the cheek and I felt her bare breast touching my arm. I was feeling a bit frustrated with the blindfold on, now that I knew Suzanne had undressed, because looking at her naked is one of my greatest pleasures. She has, as I mentioned, a statuesque body, generously endowed with sumptuous breasts and a nice round ass. Her great legs seem to go on forever, especially in the four-inch heels she always wears in "the room." My cock was beginning to stiffen at the thought of what she might look like at that moment.

"Stay still now," she said. "Don't try to touch me."

This was a game we would often play: She loves to be the boss, and I am happy to let her take charge. Slowly, she began to undress me. She removed my shirt, gliding her hands lightly over my chest, tickling the hairs around my nipples. She continued with great care, undoing my belt, untying my shoes and helping me out of them, and sliding my socks off my feet. She stopped and breathed into my ear, her tongue flicking inside it, warm and wet. "Just back up and lie down now," she whispered.

I backed up and felt the mattress behind me. As soon as I lay down, I heard her climb onto the bed. She pulled my pants down over my hips, and I felt her long hair brush against my bare thighs as she arranged my legs. Smooth hands caressed me, sliding up under the legs of my boxer shorts, fingernails lightly raking my flesh underneath them. The shorts were quickly yanked off and my cock sprang out, hard and standing straight up, begging to be touched.

My prayers were briefly answered when soft lips closed around the end of my shaft and a tongue lightly caressed the head before quickly releasing it. "You tease!" I muttered. "That's torture."

"Just relax and enjoy it," Suzanne purred.

I felt the warmth of her body near me and could smell her strong perfume—she was wearing a totally new scent that night—and I longed to reach out and stroke her. But before I could move, I felt her fasten my wrist in a tight cuff that I knew was attached to one of the bedposts. I smiled with anticipation. This was a big part of her power trip and a favorite game of mine. She quickly fastened my other wrist and did the same with each of my ankles. I lay there spread-eagled, naked and blind in the fragrant darkness, hoping desperately that Suzanne would soon take pity on my raging erection.

With great relief, I felt her position herself on the mattress. I felt her warm breath against my skin, and once again velvet lips encircled the head of my cock. Her tongue swirled around the crown, causing me to moan softly, and then she swiftly and suddenly swallowed my entire length deep into her throat. Drawing her mouth back up slowly, lips wrapped tightly around the shaft, she again flicked her tongue back and forth over the ridge. I moaned with pleasure and tried to reach out, only to be quickly reminded that my hands were bound to the bedposts.

Using only her mouth, she pumped my cock up and down violently, her efforts shaking the bed. She would follow several fast, short strokes with a long plunge, taking me fully into her throat. Then she would pull up slowly, repeat her fast strokes, and again dive down deep. It was a different technique than she normally used, and I liked it—though I wondered where she'd suddenly learned it. But my concerns were minor, as I lay back and enjoyed the sensation of my cock being slowly and lovingly devoured over and over again.

She didn't touch me except with her mouth. I felt her near me on the bed, but I couldn't understand exactly how she was positioned because her long hair wasn't touching me as it normally would. I couldn't give this much thought, however, as I became increasingly distracted by my throbbing cock and the tingling in my balls.

Suzanne must have sensed my urgency because she began to move more quickly, her mouth massaging my entire shaft. With her pace quickening, her saliva was making moist, slurping noises as she rapidly changed directions. I knew I wouldn't last much longer.

"I'm...gonna...come!" I gasped. I strained against my bonds, knowing I couldn't move but desperately trying to grab her head and hold it where it was. The best I could accomplish was to arch my back a bit and pump my hips ineffectually at her mouth. She was holding about half of my erection between her lips when my body started to spasm, and I exploded into her throat. Stream after stream of come surged out of me. After several jets of semen entered her mouth, I felt her let go and put my spurting rod against her chest, rubbing me back and forth until I had spent my load. I was a little surprised at this because Suzanne usually swallowed every drop.

As I lay there catching my breath, I began to relax, drifting into that warm afterglow and enjoying the feeling of contentment. I felt Suzanne move her hips over mine and straddle my stomach while she removed my blindfold. The scarf fell away to reveal her smiling face above me in the flickering candlelight. She was wearing her favorite outfit: only her garter belt, stockings and heels. I noticed, however, that her tits were dry, when they should have been wet and covered with semen.

"Was that good?" she cooed.

"Oh, yes!" I gasped.

Then she moved off of me, lying on her side next to me.

"Well, you'd better thank Jennifer then," she said with a nod over her shoulder.

I turned to look and there, standing at the side of the bed, was a tall, slim young woman I recognized as Suzanne's friend and protégée from the office. She was a new junior executive at the firm, just a year out of business school. Suzanne was serving as her professional mentor and now, it appeared, her personal mentor as well. This was a training exercise of which I heartily approved. Looking from one beautiful woman to the other, my mind began to race, imagining what might be in store for me. The options were lusty and many, but I willed myself to relax and surrender to their sensual plans—whatever they might be.

After I had finally overcome my initial shock, I drank in the scene with delight. Jennifer was wearing a red ribbon tied around her neck—I guess because she was my present. Drops of my semen covered her chest and chin, glistening in the dim light. Like Suzanne, she was dressed only in a garter belt and stockings, and was also as tall as my wife, well over six feet in the stiletto pumps she was wearing—but that's where the resemblance ended. Unlike my curvaceous middle-aged wife, Jennifer was a slim, coltish girl in her twenties with tiny, perky tits that seemed to be all nipples—nipples that were erect and sticking out like little rubber spikes. Her lean thighs and narrow hips made a delicious contrast to Suzanne's voluptuous form, just as her pixie-short blonde hair differed from my wife's luxurious, dark mane.

"Happy anniversary!" Jennifer said with a giggle, kissing me on the cheek. She looked at Suzanne and, with a nod from my wife, climbed onto the bed and moved up by my head. Turning her ass to me, she swung a leg over my head and straddled me so that her tight little butt was inches from my face.

"Now it's your turn, honey," I heard Suzanne say. "I'm trying to introduce Jennifer to some new activities she can try with her boyfriends. Make our guest feel welcome and rim her out a little."

With that, Jennifer lowered her sweet ass so that she was sitting on my face. I felt completely captive, my body pinned to the bed by my bonds and my head held in place between her supple thighs. I couldn't raise my head, but I poked my tongue out as far as I could and began to plant wet kisses all around her asshole. Then I ran my tongue along the line where her ass met the tops of her thighs. When I had covered as much as I could reach, she shifted her position and let me continue running my tongue up her crack. I felt my cock awakening again.

"Very good, sweetie," Suzanne said from somewhere nearby. "Somehow I knew you'd love licking her ass. Now tongue-fuck her. Let her feel your tongue sliding in and out of her ass just like a little cock."

I drove my face between her cheeks as best I could and forced my tongue into her anus. Lapping at her rosebud, I alternately rimmed around the edge and probed it with my tongue. She pushed down, nearly covering my whole face, and I began to poke my tongue in and out as quickly as I could. Jennifer was moaning and wiggling against me, and I felt proud that I could elicit such a response from this beautiful goddess.

My cock was getting harder. I wanted badly to grab it—anything to release some tension—but the way they had me bound, I could barely move a muscle.

I suddenly felt a wet, searing heat against my shaft. Suzanne had climbed onto the bed and was straddling my waist. With my cock lying erect against my stomach, my wife's cunt lips were caressing the underside of the shaft. She let them slide slowly upward, first touching my balls and then moving her wetness all the way up near the crown. I started writhing desperately, trying to push the head inside her, but it was hopeless—I was held too firmly in place. She moved around a little more, as if positioning herself, and finally came to rest with her labia caressing the middle of my shaft on each side, and my cockhead squeezed up between my stomach and her pubic hair.

I could sense some activity going on above me but, secured as I was, I couldn't see a thing except Jennifer's ass. Finally, she leaned forward a bit, and I caught a glimpse of the mirrored ceiling. My wife and her young friend, as they sat astride me, were making out furiously. They were kissing deeply, their tongues exploring each other's mouths and their hands roaming over each other's breasts. After seeing a few seconds of this, the pressure in my cock was becoming unbearable.

As I enjoyed this exquisite torture, Jennifer abruptly rose up off me and moved down to where Suzanne still sat atop me.

"You've been so good, sweetheart," Suzanne said to me with a smile. "It's time you got a little reward." Turning to Jennifer, she added, "This is one of my favorite parts."

She then raised up on her haunches and, taking my eager cock in her hand, guided it between her pussy lips. I let out a gasp as the head finally penetrated her cunt, and Suzanne paused for a second. Then she lowered her hips very slowly until she had enveloped the full length of my cock. I wanted to immediately start thrusting wildly and tried, but my bonds were so tight I could barely move my hips an inch off the bed. My wife slowly rose again until my cock reappeared, inch by inch. Adding to my sweet agony, when she reached the top, she jerked upward and let me fall out of her.

I cried out in dismay, but she simply turned to her friend and said, "Now you." My wife moved off me, and Jennifer took her place straddling my waist. She took the same approach as her mentor, reaching for my cock and guiding it to her opening. She seemed more eager than Suzanne, however, as she quickly lowered her hips and swallowed me to the hilt.

It was an amazing sensation. She was perhaps a bit wetter inside than my wife, but tighter nonetheless. Her hard nipples were pointing straight out above me, and I wanted more than anything to be able to reach up and grab them, even suck them, just touch them any way I could. As I writhed beneath her, unsuccessfully trying to move inside her even a bit, she looked me straight in the eyes, smiled devilishly, and then flexed the muscles of her vagina, seizing my shaft in a vise-like grip for a second before relaxing. My eyes rolled back in my head as I pulled against my restraints, gasping for breath. Then, like Suzanne had done, she slowly slid off me, leaving my poor cock out in the cold again.

She moved to the side, and Suzanne took her place. She repeated the same torturous technique, inserting my rock-hard dick into her cunt for a moment and releasing it, only to be replaced by Jennifer again. They repeated this over and over, switching places on my cock several times, until I was practically screaming with a combination of pleasure and disappointment.

Finally, they both slid off the mattress and stood together at the side of the bed. Their faces were flushed, and they were breathing heavily. No doubt they had enjoyed this almost as much as I had. I looked at my wife hopefully. Perhaps now I would finally get to relieve the tension in my cock.

Suzanne read my mind and gently ordered me to hold off. "Not yet, my love," she said. "Ladies first."

With that she took Jennifer's hand and led her toward the big couch on the opposite side of the room. I watched their sweet asses swaying in unison as they sashayed across the floor, their gorgeous legs looking a mile long in their heels. Suzanne positioned Jennifer on her back on the couch and then climbed atop her in the sixty-nine position. I could barely move far enough to see, but my eyeballs were popping out of my head. I was desperate to rub myself against something—anything—but my shackles made it impossible.

I could only watch as these two imperious women made passionate love. They had delayed their gratification as long as I had, and it showed in the way they hungrily devoured each other. Sounds of moaning, licking and sighing filled the room as my wife and her young protégée brought each other to orgasm again and again.

When they finally got up from the couch, I had a dull ache in my balls from being so stimulated without being able to come. I gratefully watched the two of them approach the bed. I was too dazed to even speak.

Suzanne took a vibrator from the drawer of the bedside table. Jennifer stood aside as my wife turned it on and slid the vibrator up my thigh toward my crotch. Again and again she did this from both sides. Finally, she ran the rumbling toy up the shaft of my cock, and I moaned loudly at the sensation.

"Do you like that, honey?" she said. The question did not need an answer, but I nodded my head anyway. As she continued to rub the head of the vibrator against the underside of my penis, Jennifer began stroking my shaft with her hand. "Okay, darling," Suzanne cooed as Jennifer started to jerk me off rapidly. "You can come now."

I instantly erupted. The release was incredible, and jet after jet of hot semen splashed onto my stomach. "Good boy," my wife purred. I'd never come like that before. I felt faint and dizzy, but the feeling was wonderful. Jennifer milked every last drop of fluid out of my twitching cock, but the spasms continued until I was exhausted.

As I lay there panting, Suzanne pulled Jennifer to her and thrust her tongue down her throat in a passionate kiss.

Later, after I expressed my delight to Suzanne over Jennifer's "progress," the three of us got together again—only this time Jennifer requested that she be the one shackled to the bed.

The Power of Three

Emily Nolan

It was 4:00 a.m., and I was still awake in the middle of my comfy hotel bed. Sighing, I threw my arm across my husband's body and snuggled against him. Of course, he'd been asleep for a while now, having passed out soon after reaching orgasm, as so many men are wont to do.

Settling in, I hoped I could doze off despite the fact that my heart was still racing a little, but the sound of a groan from behind me, plus the feeling of a semierect cock against my ass, thwarted my attempt. Now not only was I awake, but so was my pussy. I was certain that Ryan, an old college friend, was also asleep, and his movement was subconscious, but with my arousal mounting, I decided that someone needed to wake up. To make this happen, I spurred Ryan on by grinding my ass against his burgeoning erection.

His cock responded to my efforts by thickening and lengthening, and in the process, his erection nestled lengthwise between my cheeks. I knew he was fully awake when I felt him nuzzling the nape of my neck, so I continued moving against him to convey that I was ready for another round. He seemed to be, too, because his dick continued to stiffen until it was once again at full mast.

I really wanted to fuck him again, but I was hesitant about waking Chris because he looked so peaceful lying there beside us. With Ryan's tempting lips still trailing over my flesh, raising goose bumps wherever they touched, I gingerly lifted my arm from my husband's side and turned to face my old friend.

Ryan and I stared deep into each other's eyes before our lips met. His parted, so I slipped my tongue between them. In return, he palmed my breasts and played his fingers over my nipples, which were still so sensitive from our earlier endeavors that my body reacted instantly, giving an appreciable shudder. Reaching down, I took hold of his cock, pumping the shaft in my fist while massaging a bead of precome into the tip with my thumb. Raising my leg, I slipped his crown between my nether lips, stroking it along my slit and giving a little start each time it bumped my clit.

Ryan gasped upon feeling my wet heat and clutched my tit even harder as he attempted to slide into my slick hole. I purposefully eluded him, having too much fun masturbating with his penis. But he didn't give up easily.

Letting go of my breast, he reached down and slipped a finger between my labia, stroking me until I moaned into his mouth. That motion felt so good, I pulled away from his hand. It wasn't that I didn't want him touching me; I was now desperate to feel him inside me, and I needed something bigger than his finger.

I pushed Ryan onto his back and threw a leg across his torso to straddle him. His prick bobbed enticingly in front of me: tall, proud and ready for work. I took hold of that massive cock and rose, positioning his dick at my opening and letting the head pop inside me. As I slowly lowered myself onto his staff, I shut my eyes to revel in the feeling of being stretched wide open for the second time that night. After Ryan was fully engulfed by my cunt, I rose at the same pace and then repeated the entire process—this time a little faster.

I bounced on Ryan's dick, leaning forward so that I was crouching over him and could press my lips to his. We kissed, our tongues tangling, and I kept my eyes closed so I could concentrate on all the sensations I was feeling. And since I couldn't see anything, I first assumed it was Ryan caressing me when I felt a hand on my lower back—though, it didn't take me long to realize that hand belonged to my husband.

I opened my eyes and looked at Ryan, who winked at me. Then I glanced beside us and saw that Chris was wide awake. He also gave me a wink as he traced patterns on my skin, and the sight of his fully erect cock told me he'd been up for a while, watching me ride our old friend.

I invited Chris to join us with a smile, so he rose to his knees and kissed me. Meanwhile, Ryan grasped me by the hips and began moving me over his dick at a more leisurely pace to give my husband a chance to catch up.

As I rode Ryan, Chris's hand trailed lower, until his fingers spanned one of my asscheeks, his spit-slickened thumb working its way into my crevice. Knowing how much I like having my asshole played with, he nudged the sensitive opening and then pressed against it lightly. When I moaned, he pushed inward, stretching the muscles just wide enough for his digit.

As he stroked me from inside, I realized he could feel Ryan's movements in my other hole. This was exciting, because it was new—when we'd fucked earlier, Ryan had taken my pussy from behind while I'd sucked Chris. The thought of being doubly penetrated in this manner hadn't even occurred to me—but now it was all I could think about.

My husband kept his thumb buried in my ass while Ryan craned his neck to take one of my nipples between his teeth. I continued rising and falling on Ryan's dick, my movements easy and fluid. I felt his balls against my asscheeks whenever I touched down. After a few trips, I surmised that Chris must have been feeling them, too, which I found strangely exciting, especially because they'd had so little contact during our first encounter. This realization made me bounce up and down so erratically that Ryan had a hard time keeping his mouth on my breast. Though he managed to persevere, my husband was less successful at keeping his finger in my derriere.

Choosing a new tactic, Chris got behind me, straddling Ryan's legs. My heart raced as he bent me over even farther, until Ryan and I were face-to-face, and then he grabbed the lube from the nightstand and slathered some onto his cock. His fingers slick with gel, Chris slid one slippery digit into my asshole to get me wet and ready.

I almost came as he thrust into me, and then again when he pulled out and plunged back in, adding another digit. This time, Ryan tensed at feeling the pressure against his shaft through the thin membrane separating the two men. *If this is how we both react*, I wondered, *what'll it be like when Chris replaces his fingers with his dick?*

We were about to find out. Satisfied that I was sufficiently prepped, my husband pulled his fingers from my hole. Positioning his cock, he then pressed inward slowly, and I remained still to let him penetrate me. Ryan also stopped moving, completely entranced by the sight of me having my ass filled. Looking over my shoulder, I could see the bliss written across Chris's face, and a glance at our college buddy told me he felt the same.

With two cocks buried inside me, I held still at first, crouched on my hands and knees as the men thrust into me at the same time. The simultaneous penetration felt incredible, and I would have been ecstatic if they'd only continued in that vein. Maintaining a rhythm was difficult, however, and they decided that one man would have to push in while the other pulled out, and I'd help by not moving.

I didn't really care how we proceeded; it felt amazing no matter what we did. My pussy dripped incessantly as they pumped in and out of my holes. My breasts bounced as their movements jarred my body, and my overly sensitized nipples grazed Ryan's chest. Both he and Chris worked hard to keep sawing in and out of my cunt and anus, and it wasn't long before I felt a quivering in my belly, which spread through my entire body. When my fingers started trembling and my toes curled, I knew I was on the threshold of an incredible orgasm. Gasping, I struggled to keep myself from collapsing onto the body beneath mine, because that would have impeded Ryan's ability to keep thrusting into me.

The friction of Ryan's shaft stroking against my clit sparked my climax. I buried my face against his chest as I lost control, while he and my husband held me tightly and continued pumping into me. Soon, Chris was coming, too, as he slammed into me one last time. A moment later, Ryan's shaft quivered in my pussy as he filled me with his cream.

Demolished, we collapsed in one big heap, remaining a tangle of arms and legs as we slowly returned to our senses. Once we did, the men gently disengaged themselves, and then we settled back among the messy pile of pillows and bedsheets. After that workout, I had no trouble falling asleep, but since it was nearly dawn and a few hours from checkout time, I can say that none of us got much rest that night!

After hearing that part of my tale, you're probably wondering how all this started, how my husband and I—not necessarily all that sexually adventurous—ended up in a threesome with one of our best friends. It wasn't totally unplanned. One night, while sharing a bottle of wine, Chris and I got to talking about unrequited crushes, and I happened to mention Ryan.

"Really?" Chris said, and I could practically see the lightbulb go on over his head. "You know, the reunion is coming up, and I'm pretty sure he's single."

I was aware the reunion was coming up—a weekend affair at a swanky hotel—and apparently, so was my pussy, because it tingled at the thought of being near Ryan again. However, I couldn't see myself fucking a former love interest while my husband was somewhere else making small talk with barely remembered classmates.

"What makes you think I won't be there?" he asked, and I suddenly understood what he was getting at. When we'd talked about having a threesome before, it was always a playful conversation. This time, he was serious. And I could tell he meant business because his cock got big and hard, and the sex that followed was mind-blowing.

At the reunion a few months later, it took us about a day of reacquainting ourselves with Ryan to work up the nerve to invite him into our bed. It was my job to break the ice with a lot of flirty looks and longer-than-necessary touches. My feminine wiles must have worked because when I finally propositioned Ryan, he almost seemed like he'd been waiting for my advance. And since that evening was the last night we'd be together at the hotel, we wasted no time.

The three of us were already in our room, having retired there for what we'd simply said was a "nightcap" to celebrate a long day of festivities. When Ryan had said yes to my three-way suggestion, I moved closer to him on the couch we were sharing, wound an arm around his neck and pulled him toward me for a kiss. Meanwhile, Chris moved from his chair to the cushion behind mine and reached around to fondle my tits.

As we made out, my hand found its way to Ryan's lap, and I traced the outline of his erection through his jeans, a scenario I'd fantasized about so many times, albeit twenty years earlier. I unzipped his fly and pulled out his member, wrapping my fingers around his shaft and stroking it lightly until my husband suggested we move to the bed. We did just that, but not before we all undressed.

When Ryan was completely naked and sprawled on the mattress, I paused to admire him. His body was as beautiful as I'd always imagined, and as I ran my fingers over his chiseled chest, he took in the sight of my breasts. He leaned forward and, after kissing each of my nipples, trailed his lips downward until he reached my sex. I parted my legs, shivering when he swiped his tongue along my slit.

Chris and I both watched, entranced, as he lapped at my pussy, the first man other than my husband to do so in many years. He dragged his tongue over my quivering folds and flicked at my clit, licking me until his lips and chin were slick with my juices and the sheets beneath me were balled in my fists. It was the sort of thing that normally would have made me come rather quickly, but I was too distracted by my husband's cock, which was now in my mouth.

The oral daisy chain continued a while longer, until Ryan changed the game by thrusting a finger in my cunt. He stroked in and out of me until I yearned to feel his cock. While my husband fucked my face, I blindly tugged at Ryan, hoping he'd take the hint and replace his digit with his prick.

We were once again thwarted by logistics. In order to keep Chris in my mouth and have room for Ryan between my legs, I had to remain propped up; lying down wasn't an option. Ever the problem solver, Chris pulled his length from my lips and repositioned us so that I was on my hands and knees and Ryan was behind me, already lining up his cockhead with my cunt. Meanwhile, my husband knelt in front of me, his dick barely an inch from my face.

I captured the tip in my mouth just as Ryan grasped my hips tighter and pushed forward to pierce my pussy. Chris and Ryan both started sawing in and out at the same time, and I grabbed at the sheets to steady myself. Once stable, I swished my tongue over the underside of my husband's shaft, increasing his pleasure while increasing Ryan's by squeezing my muscles around his girth. He responded by shoving into me even harder, and I felt a thump in the pit of my belly every time his sac bounced against my asscheeks.

Threading his fingers through my hair, Chris held my head

still as he repeatedly skimmed his length over my tongue, burying himself to the balls every time. I swallowed hard, letting him feel my throat tighten around him. Then, when he pulled out, I sucked on his crown for a while, delighting in the saltiness of the precome trickling from the slit. I also delighted in the feeling of Ryan pounding into my pussy from behind. He was gripping me tightly to keep me steady, his fingers digging into my flesh as he held me by the waist.

As the men fucked me, Ryan reached beneath me and pressed his fingers to my clitoris. My entire midsection—from my stomach to my asshole—started humming. I was already seeing stars, but I had yet to really explode.

I was on the brink when Chris beat me to it. As I felt myself about to reach my peak, his shaft seemed to expand, and then I was treated to a mouthful of his cream. I started coming a second later, shaking so hard that I had difficulty gulping down his load and a lot of it ended up streaking my chin and dripping onto the sheets. Another by-product of my orgasm was that my pussy clamped around Ryan's still-thrusting member, squeezing his shaft more tightly and forcing him to thrust into me more vigorously.

Luckily, he only needed a few more pumps before he joined us in our ecstasy. Shouting his bliss, he crashed against my asscheeks one last time and then shot the contents of his balls deep into my chasm. I had never before experienced the joy I now felt at having two men pumping me full of semen at the same time, all while I was in the throes of my own orgasm. Little did I know that this experience would soon be trumped by my very first DP, only a few hours later.

For the moment, having one dick in my mouth and another in my cunt was more than enough; in fact, it was almost overwhelming.

And both men remained inside me until their balls had been depleted and my pussy was no longer contracting. Pulling out first, Chris stretched out beside me, and I leaned down to give him a kiss while our friend gave me a few last thrusts that elicited one final orgasmic shudder from me.

We invited Ryan to spend the night in our room, which is how my very first threesome was quickly followed by my very first double-fuck. Overall, it had been a memorable weekend. Hopefully, it won't be another twenty years before we see Ryan again, because now that I've experienced having two holes filled at once, I don't know if one cock will be enough to satisfy me.

Triple Play

KENDRA RICHARDSON

My husband and I are avid baseball fans, and we decided that we would finally replace our old TV with a flat-screen, high-definition model in time to watch the World Series. Matt did some research online beforehand, so when we arrived at the electronics store, we knew exactly what we wanted. I hurried to keep up with Matt's long strides as he headed straight for the home-theater area. Once there, he slowed his pace and we worked our way along the row of televisions on display, checking the specs and model numbers of each, searching for the perfect one.

Down at the end of the row, a guy in a leather jacket and baseball cap was admiring a particular set. As Matt and I moved from one TV to the next without finding the one we wanted, I got a sneaking suspicion that we would end up at the same model the other customer was interested in. Sure enough, that's exactly what happened. "Here we go, Kendra," said Matt as he inspected the stylish flat-screen TV and its tag.

"Oh, you guys like this one, too?" the stranger asked, turning to us with a handsome smile.

My breath caught in my throat. He was very good-looking, with short, sandy-colored hair, a square jaw and a fit, athletic build. His baseball hat was the fitted kind, not adjustable, a sure sign of a die-hard fan. He had an outgoing manner, and I liked him instantly. In the moments that followed, it was clear that Matt did, too.

"Yes, we've had our eye on this model," Matt explained. "The World Series is going to look great on this baby."

The man's face lit up. "That's for sure. I was thinking the same thing." He laughed, looking from me to Matt and back again. "Watching the series on my old twenty-four-inch TV just won't cut it this year." I could see in his blue eyes that he found me attractive.

A salesman came over, looking embarrassed. "I hope you don't both want this one, because I'm pretty sure we only have the display model left," he said, somewhat sheepishly.

There was an awkward silence. Matt looked at the salesman, then at me, then at our new friend. "Well, why don't you go check to be sure," he said. The sales guy nodded and headed off. While we waited for him, the three of us talked baseball—the just-concluded season, the playoffs, the teams and players we liked. All the while, I got hotter and hotter for this man, whose name, we learned, was Jason. He was almost Matt's height, but a little slimmer and probably half a dozen years younger. He and Matt were soon clicking like old buddies, and I felt a surge of horniness at Jason's unmistakable desire for me. We were all hitting it off so well that we almost didn't notice the salesman's return.

"Sorry, it's like I said," the guy apologized. "I only have this one unit." This was not good news—or was it? I was getting an idea that made my palms sweaty and my heart beat faster. You see, Matt and I enjoy pushing the boundaries of our sexual relationship. We discovered a while back that we especially love three-way sex; we've had both men and women join us for some incredibly exciting, unforgettable encounters. Now, watching and talking with Jason, I came to the conclusion that he would be game for some three-way action with me and Matt.

"Look, we can find another TV," Matt was saying. My husband is many things—smart, funny, great in bed—but he's not selfish. Nor is he blind; I knew he had picked up on the sexual attraction between Jason and me. I caught him looking at me with an *I know what you're thinking* smile, and I could tell he was open to a threesome with Jason.

"No, you guys take the TV," our new friend said earnestly. "To tell you the truth, it's really too much for my budget anyway."

I sensed this was an honest remark, but I wasn't prepared to let Jason off the hook so easily. "How about this," I piped up, laying my hand on Jason's arm. "We'll take it, but only if you'll come watch game one at our place."

Jason smiled broadly. "Sure, that would be great!" he said. We exchanged phone numbers and gave him our address. Ten minutes and one new TV later, we bid goodbye to Jason until the first game of the series.

Five long days later, our doorbell rang about an hour before game time. Matt went to answer it and came back to the living room with Jason, whose eyes grew wide when he saw me. I was wearing my shortest shorts and a replica team baseball jersey with the top three buttons undone, so that my full breasts were on display. Jason swallowed hard, and I almost giggled. I caught a whiff of his sexy cologne as he gave me a peck on the cheek.

Matt made margaritas for everyone and then took the easy chair, while I sat down next to Jason on the couch. The TV was showing pregame ceremonies, but I must confess, baseball was no longer foremost on my mind. As we talked and got to know Jason better, I felt an exciting vibe of sexual tension in the room. I flirted brazenly with our guest, who enjoyed my overtures but was obviously unsure how to react. I excused myself to bring our empty glasses back to the kitchen, giving Matt an opportunity to talk plainly with Jason.

When I returned, Jason's smile had taken on an animated, almost incredulous quality, like he had just found out he'd won the lottery. "Matt says"—he swallowed and his voice dropped to a hush—"he says you'd like us both to fuck you, Kendra. Is that right? Because, frankly, I'd love to."

"Then what are we waiting for?" I replied, feeling my pulse race. I knelt on the couch close beside Jason and looked deep into his eyes as I slowly unzipped his fly. Behind me, Matt started to undress. Jason eased back into the couch and let me pull out his cock, which was quite impressive—long, stout and heavily veined, with a thatch of light brown pubic hair at the base. I lowered my head and filled my mouth with the helmet-shaped cap. It felt large and dense, a fleshy knob of sensitive nerve endings that quivered against my palate. I fastened my lips around the shaft, just below the glans, and sucked gently at first, then more urgently. Jason sighed with pleasure, and I felt his manhood grow even harder. He ran his hand through my hair, holding it back from my face as I swallowed his tool.

Matt knelt on the couch behind me, pulled off my shorts and stroked my ass, which was high in the air. He pushed my knees wider and dipped his face into my smooth cleft. I could feel every detail of his lips and chin against my swollen nether lips. As Matt slipped his tongue into my folds, I remained bent over Jason's lap, earnestly licking and sucking his cock. Jason moaned and moved his hips, increasing the friction of my lips on his pole. I relaxed my throat and took more of his rod into my mouth, until I had engulfed most of its length. Then I waited a beat, letting the vibrations in my throat tease Jason, before pulling back to the top of his cock again. His fingers coiled in my hair, twisting my blonde tresses in response to the play of my tongue along the underside of his prick. He slipped his other hand into my open shirt and toyed with my breasts, which swayed forward and back as I bobbed over his length.

Meanwhile, Matt continued to swirl his tongue in my cunt, making me gasp every time he flicked my clit. He stopped for a second to peel me open with his fingertips, admiring the mouth of my sex and my swollen bud. Then he renewed his tongue attack, making me sloppy back there with a mix of his saliva and my juices. The pleasure was intense, and I was finding it hard to keep my mouth on Jason's cock. I had a moment's relief when my husband, yielding to his own need, suddenly straightened up and placed his cock at the opening of my cunt. Then he grasped the globes of my ass with both hands and leaned into me, filling me in one sublime thrust. I cried out with pleasure, momentarily losing my grip on Jason's penis.

Grabbing hold of that thick spike again, I let Jason guide my head down until my lips encircled his shaft once more. Behind me, Matt was sliding in and out of my slick channel with an easy rhythm, but he was just getting started. I knew his insouciance belied a storm of excitement and anticipation that was roiling inside him. With each plunge into my sex, his cock seemed to swell, growing a little longer and thicker inside me. He increased the pace of his thrusts, grunting each time his heavy ball sac slapped against my vulva. The impacts sent sparks of pleasure coursing through my body and propelled me forward against Jason's cock. Leaning over my shoulder as he pumped against my ass, Matt watched me work at Jason's tumescence. I knew my husband was taking his own vicarious pleasure in the sight of his wife enthusiastically sucking off another man. Imagining the scene through Matt's eyes ramped up my own passion, making my whole body flutter with arousal.

It was incredibly satisfying to be penetrated at both ends like that. Apparently, the guys were more than a little excited, too, for as I tasted precome on the tip of Jason's cock, Matt stiffened behind me and sent a stream of ejaculate deep into my cunt. I felt his cock pulsing inside me as it discharged its load of warm cream. "That's it, honey, fill me up!" I cried, looking back at Matt over my shoulder while running my hand up and down Jason's pole. Eventually Matt's spasms subsided and his softening cock slipped out of me, but I knew he would quickly recover and be ready for more action. I wasn't sure about Jason, so I decided not to let him come just yet. I was eager to make our fun last as long as possible, and I was sure that both men felt the same way.

Letting go of Jason, I turned around on the couch and lay between my two lovers, with my head practically in Matt's lap and my thighs spread open for Jason's magnificent prick. Knowing my nude body was totally on display for both of them filled me with new waves of lust. "Take me here," I purred to Jason, regarding him with half-closed eyes and using two fingers to peel back the lips of my pussy. Without waiting for his reaction, I reached for my husband's cock, which was already stiffening up again. My own juices were all over the shaft, making it shine in the lamplight. Greedily I lapped along its underside, feeling the skin grow more taut by the second. I started at the bristly root and moved up the shaft to the head, then back again. Matt's perineum was in easy reach of my tongue, so I traced wet circles there, then moved across the wrinkly skin of his balls, too. His scent, intermingled with mine, was intoxicating.

Down at the other end of my body, Jason grabbed hold of my upraised thighs, planted one foot on the floor beside the couch, and pulled my hips toward him. A moment later he shoved into my sex, taking my breath away. His cock was a stranger to my cunt, its contours thrillingly unfamiliar. I could feel every detail of its shape and thickness as it burrowed deep into me, seeking my sexual core. My thigh muscles flexed involuntarily and my ass lifted off the couch when Jason's root smacked against my clit. I bucked against him, encouraging him to go faster. Reaching under me, he grasped my buttocks and then really started to pound into me, like a man possessed. His balls slapped against the cheeks of my ass with a salacious smacking sound, and beads of sweat from his forehead spattered my breasts and belly.

Watching all this, Matt made a sound of satisfaction deep in his throat. He turned to gaze down at me, his face filled with passion. Taking hold of his cock, he aimed it downward and fed it, inch by inch, into my hungry mouth. When about half his length had disappeared between my lips, he stopped and let me take over. With feverish delight, I arched my neck a little and took more of him, until his glans touched the back of my throat. Compared to Jason's meaty truncheon,

Matt's cock felt smoother against my tongue, straighter and more polished. I loved them both. Matt began raising and lowering himself above my face, fucking my mouth. His eyes returned to the sight of Jason's spike as it plowed in and out of my dripping hole. I reached around Matt's waist and grabbed his ass as a sudden rush of pleasure surged up from my center, making me abandon my husband's cock. "Oh god, I'm coming!" I cried, reveling in the blissful sensations that wracked my body.

Jason held my thighs fast against his chest, and I think he almost came then, but with a Herculean effort, he pulled out of my cunt, gripping the base of his cock tightly. "Turn over," he suggested, and I happily complied, getting onto my hands and knees so he could penetrate me doggie-style.

With frantic passion he aimed his cock at my dripping cunt and slammed into me. His prick felt like it was on fire as it thrust in and out of my molten core. Soon I felt like I was on the verge of coming again. Jason leaned over me, reached around and filled his hands with my breasts. His wild fingers tweaked and pinched my nipples, amplifying the ripples of pleasure coursing through my entire being.

Matt watched us for a moment, transfixed. Then he crawled underneath us so that his face was directly below my cunt. The sight filling his vision must have been amazing: my blonde pubic bush matted with sex juice, Jason's fat prick powering in and out of my pink channel, his pendulous balls spanking smartly against my slick labia. Matt's cock, harder than ever, was right there in front of me, standing up tall and proud from his groin, so I curled my palm around it and began pumping my hand up and down the shaft. At the same time, I felt Matt's warm breath on my pussy, followed by the touch of his fingers on my distended clit. Then came the additional sensation of his tongue, featherlight but insistent, as he licked at my sex—and at Jason's, too. Boldly he worked his warm tongue into my folds where Jason's cock was pumping wildly into me. Jason's initial cry of surprise gave way to a guttural moan of deep pleasure. His hands tightened on my breasts and his thrusts into my sex became stronger, almost feral. Encouraged, Matt plied our sticky juncture with greater zest, spreading me open so he could stroke and lick Jason's cock as it rocketed back and forth in my vagina. He lapped at us both, tasting us and spreading his saliva from my swollen clit to Jason's swaying balls. Jason was going insane with excitement, and I was, too, pushing back and grinding my cunt against him. The passionate sounds of our torrid three-way union echoed through the house.

When my unruly palpitations uncoupled me from Jason's dick, Matt took hold of the other man's twitching phallus and aimed it a bit higher, toward my tiniest hole. The idea of having Jason finish in my backside while Matt looked on from below sent a surge of adrenaline through my body. "Yes, that's it!" I said in a strained, husky voice. "Shoot your load in my ass, Jason!" He was already entering me, pushing his slick member through my sphincter. Matt curved one hand against my pussy, rubbing fiercely, and used his other hand to help guide Jason's prick farther into my asshole. I was fully impaled in no time, and the sensation was so intense, so sublime, that I finally slipped over the brink of ecstasy. Eyes closed, I lowered my face into my husband's pubic hair and held my ass up high for Jason. He pulled out of my rear just to the head of his cock, then plunged back in to the hilt, and I saw stars. With a carnal bellow that reverberated through the room, Jason came with me, his body jolting uncontrollably against me. His throbbing cock felt huge in my ass as it spat hot semen up my back channel. A string of successive climaxes ripped through me from the inside out. Jason withdrew from my asshole in time to decorate my buttocks with a few last spurts of warm cream, which he sensually rubbed into my skin.

Somehow I managed to keep my hand on Matt's quivering prick. My palm flew up and down, fed by the force of my orgasm, and suddenly Matt's cock erupted wildly, shooting his white cream into the air like a geyser. I let the fluid coat my hand and then licked my fingers clean.

As the room quieted and we all regained our breath, we heard the play-by-play broadcaster on the TV saying, "We move to the fourth inning, the score tied at one..."

Jason, Matt and I looked at each other and burst into laughter.

"I guess we've missed some of the game," I said.

"It was worth it," Jason replied, grinning.

"Well, it's only Game One," Matt told him. "Would you like to come back and join us for the rest of the series?"

"Count on it," Jason said, and I knew he would return for more fun and games.

Threesome by the Book

Sommer Marsden

When I hit my thirtieth birthday, Chris asked me if there were any fantasies he could help make come true. We were extremely open in expressing our wants and needs, but there was one fantasy I'd been keeping close to my chest.

I studied his kind face and then brushed my finger over his lower lip. His tongue darted out automatically to touch my fingertip. Heat and desire curled in my belly and settled lower in a mere heartbeat.

"I have one," I confessed. I dragged my fingers up the sharpness of his cheekbone and stroked his eyebrow so he shut his eyes. Then I combed my fingers through his light brown hair, liking the soft feel.

"Why haven't you told me?" he asked. But then he hummed with pleasure because I'd touched the front of his jeans. Just thinking of confessing my heart's desire had me revved up. My pussy was wet, my nipples hard. The excitement that surged inside me every time we were intimate was ever ready and utterly present.

"I don't know. I guess I didn't think about it…until you asked. It seems so completely ridiculous. The things you see in movies but not in real life."

He opened his bright blue eyes and regarded me patiently. "You're getting me all worked up and haven't even told me what *it* is."

"Another woman," I said. "With us."

He cocked an eyebrow and took my wrist in his hand. His big fingers pinning my pulse beneath his grip made my pussy clench. I knew this conversation was going to end in fucking, but somehow the anticipation was as delicious as the conclusion would be.

"Isn't the fantasy *du jour* another man? Because if you're afraid to tell me…"

I shook my head before he could even finish the sentence.

"Nope. Not changing it for you. It truly is my fantasy."

As I talked, he put his hands on my hips and lifted my short cotton skirt up my thighs. When he exposed my candy-cane-striped panties, he smiled.

"And why a woman?"

I shrugged and tried to continue breathing as he slipped his fingers beneath the waistband of my panties and forced them down. I was so wet I marveled at the sensation. "Curiosity, I guess. I've never been kissed by another woman."

His fingers dragged slowly across my already swollen clit. He pushed his hand down farther and slid a finger inside me. My hips shot forward, and I gasped softly. Then I laughed.

"Not even a single kiss? Not even a long time ago as an experiment?" His voice was a deep rumble that turned me on incredibly.

"Nope. And I've often wondered," I went on, "what it would feel like to have a woman's mouth on my pussy. Her tongue. What she would do and *how* she would do it, as opposed to a man." I looked at him and touched his face again. "No offense."

"Jesus. No offense taken, baby."

He dropped to his knees, and my heart stuttered. My skirt and my panties were now around my ankles, and he put his hands on my feet and leaned in. His breath hit me first, warm and soft, and then his tongue invaded me. I felt as if I'd buckle, so I put my hands on his broad shoulders to steady myself.

"What's this?" I asked with a sigh. "I thought I was confessing to you."

"Keep going," he mumbled. His lips and tongue were working me so that my mind had grown fuzzy, but I tried my best.

"I want to know what a woman's hands would feel like on me. And I'd like to know what it would look like..." I paused.

He sucked my clit, and then soothed it with his tongue. His eyes were open and regarding me. His stare was penetrating.

"What it would look like to what?"

"See you with her. If you could get into that. I don't know if I'd feel jealous or turned on or what. Probably both." I laughed. "It turns me on to think of it. But—"

"What?" He sucked my clit again, and my brain went blank.

I shook my head. "Nothing. It sounds selfish."

He lapped at me, taking my moisture and adding his own. His hands skated up my inner thighs, which promptly began to tremble.

He pushed a few fingers inside my pussy and started to thrust them in and out.

"Tell me," he demanded.

"Mostly me," I said. "Obviously, it's my fantasy so it's mostly about...me."

He thrust his fingers deeper, flexed them, brought me up the highest peak and then he dropped me off. He licked my clitoris relentlessly until I was coming, grasping his shoulders as if he could save me.

My knees dipped, and he took advantage of the movement by grabbing my wrist and tugging me down to the floor with him. He removed my blouse and then my bra. His mouth was warm and sweet on my nipples. I raised my hips and wrapped my legs around his waist. My pussy opened to him, and he pounded into me fast and hard. My body clutched at him, and pleasure—swift and wonderful—flooded my system. Gorgeous shades of purple, pink and red swarmed behind my eyelids. I hummed and drove my body up to meet his.

Chris pressed his mouth to my ear and whispered, "It should be about you. All about you. Whatever you want, I want to give it to you."

Love made my chest ache because I knew he meant it—100 percent.

He hiked my hips up high and angled me so that every single inch of his cock brushed my most sensitive places. I clenched my pussy around him, triggering a growl. "I wish I knew someone," he said, his face serious. He was so close, and I was right there with him.

"I have a person in mind," I confessed. "At least fantasy-wise."

"Who?" he demanded, his rhythm becoming faster and more intense. My back scooted across the carpet in the brightly lit living room. We were screwing right there in the middle of the floor like newlyweds.

"Ms. Kadrey."

He paused, staring down at me. The pause only served to heighten my pleasure. I could feel my cunt beating in time with my heart.

"The librarian?"

I nodded, moving my hips greedily so that we both groaned. It felt so good. Nearly too good.

"She's in her late forties," he responded.

"So?" I laughed. "She's a repressed sex pot. And smart, too."

"You want us to fuck Ms. Kadrey?"

I nodded.

He hung his head and grunted, then his hips were in motion. "Jesus Christ," Chris said. "I'm going to come."

And as usual, I was right there with him.

I couldn't tell what he was going to do. I'd have been a nervous wreck, addressing a sexy older woman and propositioning her for a threeway. I'd never have been able to utter the words. But my husband is well spoken and brave beyond measure.

He'd texted me to say that he'd be stopping in the library after work. He was going to talk to Ms. Kadrey, if she was there.

Part of me hoped beyond explanation that she was there. Part of me was terrified she'd be working. I wanted this ménage à trois more and more as we discussed it. The confession part had added considerable fuel to my fantasy fire. I'd had several dreams about what it would be like to have Ms. Kadrey in our bed. What it would be like to have her elegant hands, always bejeweled in fantastical rings, gliding across my skin. Parting my pussy lips. Stroking me to orgasm.

I pictured her lips, always painted a vibrant red, on my pussy. It was all too easy to imagine her taking charge. The persona she emits is one of confidence and control.

I insinuated my hand into my slacks and breached my panties. I painted the moisture waiting for me there over my throbbing clit. I let my imagination run wild. Ms. Kadrey sucking me. Licking me. Ms. Kadrey with her face buried between my legs, eating me as my husband fucked her, driving her forward over and over again until the inevitable conclusion.

I delivered one more tender stroke to my clitoris, and the orgasm shook me to my bones. It skittered through me and stole my breath. I heard Chris's car door slam and hurriedly tried to put myself back together, though I knew there would be no hiding the spots of color in my cheeks or how flustered I felt.

His key turned in the door, and I stood there, frozen like a deer in headlights, awaiting the verdict. He walked in and a grin lit his face. "What have *you* been doing?"

"Nothing," I lied.

He was on me then, gathering my right hand in his and pulling it to his face. "The scent of your fingers says otherwise."

"Okay, you caught me," I blurted. "And?"

"And?" He mocked me, torturing me on purpose for fibbing.

"She said?"

He smiled even more broadly, the sight going straight to the center of me. He kissed me once, almost chastely, which drove me crazy—and he knew it.

"Hazel said yes."

"Hazel?"

"That's her name."

"I never knew."

"Me, either," he said. "But since we invited her into our bed, I figured I'd ask."

"She really said yes?" I sat on the sofa, feeling weak in the knees.

"Lucky for me, it was dead in there. I told her I had an unorthodox request. She said shoot. So I shot. I laid it all out for her, and much to my shock and amazement…she agreed."

"When?" I queried, hands shaking. We were going to make it happen.

"Tomorrow night. I invited her to come for a drink and then stay for a come." He chuckled, amusing himself.

"Wow."

"Yes, wow," he said. "Now stand up."

"What?"

He took my hand, and I stood as he said, "I want to pick up where you left off. You started without me, but I can make up for lost time."

He was right. And he did.

Hazel showed up at our home the next evening in one of her signature wrap dresses. A taupe-and-black number in a pattern resembling brocade. The collar and cuffs were solid black, and her shoes matched the taupe tone perfectly. Her dark blonde hair was artfully arranged in a French twist, her lipstick was red and in her elegant hands she held a dozen roses and a bottle of prosecco.

"Gifts?" I murmured, nervously. "Shouldn't we be giving *you* gifts?" I took the roses with shaking hands.

She smiled and cocked her head. A single lock of hair slipped down and brushed her cheek. "Oh, but you are. I haven't had some good old-fashioned dirty fun in a long time."

Her voice was low and soothing and made me smile. Fitting, obviously, for a librarian. I handed Chris the wine and let him go about opening the bottle.

"Were you shocked?" I asked, trying my best at small talk. It was hard not to focus on the generous but tasteful cleavage the dress showed off. Her waist was a bit softer than it probably once had been, but the lushness of her body made me want to touch her more.

I imagined her sweetly perfumed, touching me. Naked. On her knees. Chris behind her.

My cheeks reddened; I could feel the heat. And she caught it, too, because she reached up and ran her fingertips over the red blossoms of my excitement.

"A little. But just at how bold your husband was without really knowing me. He loves you very much."

I nodded, swallowing hard, as her hand slid down my neck, eliciting goose bumps as it traveled. I felt my nipples spike in my bra and my pussy clench wetly with arousal. I was barely breathing and tiny white dots swam in my vision.

"I hope you don't think me bold, but now that I'm here, I think the wine can wait. Like I said, it's been a long while for me. Too long.

I'm always busy and some would say"—she laughed in self-deprecation—"a bit of a fusspot when it comes to lovers. But something about the sincere, forthright nature of your man made me decide to go for it."

That hand traversed my shoulder, detoured over my collarbone and finally slipped down to caress my breast. Her thumb found my nipple with ease. Her touch was everything I'd imagined it would be. She hefted my left breast in her hand and ran her thumb over my nipple again.

Chris walked in with the wine and froze. "Are we skipping wine?" he asked.

I stared at her, half-mesmerized by the fact that she was there and touching me. Hazel smiled and nodded slowly. "I do believe we're skipping wine. Or rather," she said, glancing up at Chris, "postponing it."

She moved closer to me, and I could feel Chris, there in the doorway, holding his breath. Our living room was furnished with a large L-shaped sofa, a chaise lounge and two big overstuffed chairs. It was at the back of the house and looked out on a yard with a privacy fence. I was perfectly comfortable with our threesome developing there. I preferred it even, seeing as the bedroom felt like too much of a space imprinted with my energy and Chris's. The living room was where we entertained. And that day, we were entertaining Hazel.

She unbuttoned my navy-blue dress, one silver button at a time. She kept those warm brown eyes on me, and when I was least expecting it, she leaned in to kiss me on the mouth. Her lips were firm and warm and perfectly in control.

My panties grew wetter, and my legs quivered enough for me to worry about falling on my ass. I smiled, and she laughed.

"You're very pretty. I've noticed you before." She pushed my filleted dress back and swept down—somehow still elegant—to tug at my demi-cup bra and take one of my nipples into her mouth. What felt like an electric current ran beneath my skin, and I found myself pushing my hips forward as she sucked that tender nub of flesh. She took advantage of my state by cupping my mound through my panties.

My eyes shot to Chris, and I saw him leaning against the wall, his hand nonchalantly on his hard-on. He watched every move with avid eyes and a half smile on his handsome face.

Finally, when I thought I might expire, Hazel pushed my dress all the way down until it puddled at my feet. I stepped free of the fabric as she took control and unhooked my bra and then slid my knickers down. I kicked those off and stood before her utterly nude.

"Like I said," she whispered. "You're very pretty. How about you sit on the sofa."

"I was wondering…I don't know what Chris said, but—"

"Oh, me and you, him and me. Him and me and you." She winked. "Don't worry. We'll get there."

I inhaled deeply and exhaled just as heartily. Having her in charge was nice—it helped me relax.

I sat back on the sofa, and Hazel moved toward me slowly. She sank to her knees, and my body shivered from head to toe at seeing my fantasy coming to life. She dragged her fingernails down my belly and my sides, and my muscles jumped. She caressed my inner thighs, and I heard Chris make a noise. He began to unbutton his shirt as Hazel descended on me slowly, allowing me to watch her every move. Her tongue was small and rosy, and she arched it to deliver a single lick to my clitoris.

Another tremble worked through me, and I gripped the tan sofa cushions in my hands. She licked me again before pausing to suck my clit between her lips. Captured in the velvet heat, she nudged it repeatedly until I was writhing, despite my best efforts to stay still.

She began to pet my inner thighs again, and I mentally begged her to put her fingers in me. She obeyed my unspoken request and slipped a digit into my dripping slit. I raised my hips again, my concentration only broken when I heard the snap of a condom as Chris sheathed himself.

He moved behind Hazel and hiked her dress up. I guessed that he pushed a finger inside her to test her wetness when she let her big brown eyes drift shut. Then Chris began the erotic dance of undressing our guest.

When he took her bra off, her breasts spilled free, and despite the distraction of the constant licks and whirls of her tongue, I noticed her nipples were large and very pink. A pale pink that reminded me of roses.

Soon she was entirely nude and adding two more fingers to my cunt. She expertly manipulated me until I was gasping for air, curling her fingers over and over again until I was coming. I stroked her hair, enjoying the silken texture beneath my fingers.

Chris entered her, gripping her hips in his hands. Them on the floor, me on the sofa. He began with a slow, even thrust that drove her forward against my pussy. Her lips nudging me that way, just after an orgasm, drove me mad. I watched him fucking her and reached down to cup her heavy breasts in my hands. I pinched her nipples, and she inhaled sharply.

"Again," Hazel said, and I obeyed. I pinched her now-hard

nipples until her face reflected her pleasure clearly. Chris drove into her harder, and her tongue was at me again. He rotated his trim hips in the way that always makes me come. Hazel slammed her body back to take him; she suckled at my tender clit and then licked me lazily. The easy rhythm was precisely what I needed.

Chris sucked on his thumb and slipped the wet tip into her ass as he bucked behind her. He slowed and then sped up, keeping her off balance. Her mouth never stopped moving on my pussy lips and clitoris. I thrust up to grind my cunt against her lips, and when I came, I cried out loudly, unapologetic.

She came with me, the sound of my climax triggering hers.

"I think I'd like for you to go down on me," she said, smiling. She was calm, cool and collected, tucking that stray strand of hair behind her ear.

I nodded, waiting for the sensation to come back into my limbs. When I stood on shaky legs, I saw Chris remove the condom. He winked at me, and my heart leapt. We were fulfilling this fantasy together, and it was more than I'd anticipated.

Hazel took her place almost primly, spreading her trim thighs. I ran my hands up and down her legs, feeling the softness of her skin. I spread her pussy lips and studied her rosy cunt. I blew across it even as Chris levered me forward and entered me.

My cunt gripped around him, eager to be filled. I leaned in and smelled the musky but sweet scent of her. I touched my tongue to her pussy, and she practically purred. Subtle flavors filled my mouth, and I began to lick. I concentrated on delivering to her the pleasure she'd given me. I did all the things with my tongue that I adore having Chris do to me.

I licked her swollen clit, holding my tongue pressed flat and broad, until she began to wriggle. Then I tickled her clit with the rigid tip. When that triggered a response, I sucked her button. Her breath rushed out of her quickly, and I almost smiled, feeling victorious.

Every time Chris thrust into me, he brought me closer to another orgasm. She reached down and stroked my nipple with a featherlight touch. I whimpered against her pussy, never pausing with my tongue. I pushed my fingers into her and reveled in the grip of her cunt.

"Jesus, babe," Chris said. He was so close.

I nodded, suckling her and fucking her with my fingers. She moved quickly and grabbed some of my hair, tugging it as she came with a long, low sigh.

I had done that, and the knowledge set me off. I tightened my cunt around Chris and embraced my orgasm. Pleasure rushed over me as he cursed softly and followed suit.

When my senses swam back to me and my focus returned, Hazel was watching me, stroking my hair.

She glanced up at my husband and smiled. "Now," she said, "about that wine."

Exotic Ecstasy

Kailani Cooper

"Aloha, enjoy the luau." As I put the flower lei around the young man's neck, he glanced at my cleavage. When you have a figure like mine and you're wearing nothing above the waist but a pair of seashells over your breasts, you get plenty of looks. My handmade ti-leaf skirt was pretty racy, too. I wore it precariously low on my hips. Whenever I moved, the leaves swished this way and that, offering provocative glimpses of my thighs.

I'm a hula dancer at a Hawaiian luau. At that moment, my job was to welcome guests to our outdoor seating area near the beach. "Aloha, enjoy the show," I said as the next couple in line stepped up. When I started to place a lei over the man's head, we recognized each other.

"It's you!" Andre exclaimed, grinning. "From this morning."

His wife, Celia, smiled warmly. "Hello again," she said.

Their accents—something Mediterranean—were just as appealing as they'd been during our brief encounter on the beach. "Oh! Hi," I stammered, feeling my insides turn tingly warm. "Small island."

I had been taking my morning jog on Kaanapali Beach when I came upon a shirtless, deeply tanned man in board shorts taking photos of a bikini-clad woman as she posed knee-deep in the surf. They were trading a lot of banter, laughing and thoroughly enjoying themselves. *There's an attractive couple,* I thought to myself. *Probably honeymooners.* And then, *I wonder if they're into threesomes.*

You see, I'd recently had three-way sex. It was completely spontaneous and so mind-blowingly good that ever since, I'd been on the lookout for an opportunity to do it again. When I saw the couple on the beach, I couldn't help wondering. They were magnetic.

They took note of me, too. No surprise there. My string bikini turns heads as much as my hula outfit. For a moment I saw myself through their eyes: long black hair, exotic features, golden tan, skimpy swimsuit, curvaceous figure.

"Would you take a picture of Celia and me together?" the man called out.

"Sure." I came over and took the camera from his outstretched hand. His longish hair was light brown, his eyes hazel. He was lean and muscular, with nice definition to his abs and chest. The woman was in good shape, too, slender and very pretty, with hair almost as dark as mine. They struck a pose, holding each other and looking sexy as the waves crashed about their feet. I felt a quiver of sexual desire in my core as I snapped a couple of shots.

The man suddenly swept up his companion in his arms. "Andre!" she exclaimed, laughing.

I pressed the shutter button again, admiring the knotted muscles in Andre's arms and the shapely contours of Celia's dangling legs.

Satisfied at last, he set her down. The whole thing had only taken a minute or two, but I felt drawn to this couple. I couldn't make myself jog away at first, nor could I deny the physical attraction I was feeling toward both of them.

Andre said, "Thank you, uh…"

"Kailani," I replied.

He smiled. "You're beautiful."

"Don't mind my husband," Celia said. "He can be so forward." But I saw in the way she looked at me that she agreed with Andre's assessment. The tingle of arousal inside me intensified.

"Thanks," I said. "Here's your camera."

And that's how it ended, but there they were again, as if we were fated to come together. Andre wore a white linen shirt and tan pants. Celia wore a floral-print dress that flattered her figure. Why did they make me feel so damn horny?

"Aloha," I said, placing a lei around Celia's neck.

She kissed my cheek. "Can't wait to see you dance."

Celia and Andre continued on to their seats, but not before I caught a look from them both that really made my cunt pulse with excitement.

The staff lit torches and brought out a dozen Polynesian dishes for dinner as the sun touched the sea behind us. Soon the music started, and it was time for me to perform. Andre and Celia, sitting at a front-row table, seemed to have eyes only for me, despite the other dancers who frequently shared the stage. Their rapt attention made me dance with extra passion.

When the MC invited all newlyweds up to the stage, Andre and Celia came up with about a dozen others. We guided them through a minute or two of hula moves, much to the crowd's amusement. Celia took the opportunity to whisper in my ear, "Will you meet us later?"

I nodded and squeezed her hand.

After the gaggle of honeymooners was led off the stage, I performed one last dance, a particularly sensual one about Pele, the Hawaiian Goddess of Fire. Then I gave way to our fire dancer, who wrapped up the luau with dramatic twirls of his flaming torch.

As everyone filed toward the exits, I lingered near the stage, looking for my two admirers. Someone tapped me on the shoulder. I turned, and there they were.

"How'd you like the show?" I asked.

"Extraordinario!" Celia beamed.

"But the mai tais, on the other hand…" Andre made a face, but his eyes twinkled humorously.

"Andre, don't be rude."

"What? She didn't make the drinks."

I laughed. "No, I didn't. And you're right. For a real drink, try the tiki bar on the beach." I pointed toward a bamboo-sided structure in the distance. "You can walk from here."

"Have one with us?" Celia asked.

"I'd love to."

As we walked on the sand, Andre said, "'Kailani.' What's it mean?"

"Sea and sky," I explained.

"That's lovely," Celia said, taking my hand.

At the tiki bar, we sat at a small table and ordered drinks. That's when I realized I had forgotten to change out of my hula costume. Maybe I had "forgotten" on purpose. I always felt sexy in it, and at that moment, that's exactly what I wanted.

As we sipped our drinks and talked, I learned they were from Lisbon and had lived together for seven years before tying the knot a week ago. At last, Celia put her hand on mine and said, "Andre and I were hoping that on this trip, we might experience…something new."

My heart pounded. "Like what?"

"Like," said Andre, ever the direct one, "a ménage à trois." He studied me closely. "You're not surprised."

"No," I answered. "Turned on, yes—definitely." I took a deep breath.

"Then?" Celia inquired hopefully.

I finished my drink. "Let me show you something."

Andre dropped some bills on the table, then he and Celia followed me as I headed down the beach, away from the lights and people. Eventually, I stopped and pointed out over the ocean, where a strange glow illuminated the horizon.

"Look," I said.

Impossibly large and silvery-pink, the moon seemed to emerge from the sea itself. Celia gasped; Andre stood transfixed. As the moon rose into the sky, I felt my ardor rise with it. I took Andre's hand in my left and Celia's in my right. Together we watched until the entire moon was visible, almost too bright to look at. Then I turned to my companions.

Andre answered the call first, pressing his lips to mine with a hunger that rivaled my own. When Celia took his place, kissing me with pillowy-soft lips, Andre knelt in the sand and put his head under my skirt. He pulled down my underwear and caressed my triangle of wispy black pubes for a moment. Then I gasped against Celia's mouth as Andre planted a kiss right on my vulva. He ran his hands up my thighs to my labia and peeled me open. I quivered from head to foot as his tongue dipped inside me, probing deep. His hands went around to my ass, and he held me tightly to his face. My juices were flowing copiously. Andre licked them up, his wet slurping noises mixed with his moans of satisfaction.

Meanwhile, Celia and I continued to twine our tongues together. Her actions had been tentative at first, until I responded eagerly. Then she let herself go, kissing me with a passion so strong that my whole body felt like it was on fire. She reached around my neck and untied the string there, then did the same at the one around my back. My seashell top fell away, and Celia quickly pressed her hands to my breasts. At first she stroked my boobs lightly, working my nipples into stiff points with a feathery touch. Then she began to palm my tits more aggressively, as if their feel and shape were secrets she had to grasp while she had the chance. But I wasn't going anywhere. My breasts, my cunt, my whole body was for Celia and Andre, just as I knew theirs were for me, and for each other.

Celia bent and closed her lips over each of my nipples in turn, fanning the flames of my desire. I stroked her hair and pushed my breasts toward her while Andre, beneath my hula skirt, continued to take his fill of my sex. He lapped at my hole and sucked on my clit like a man on a mission. Perhaps thirty seconds later, I felt the orgasm roll up through my belly and burst exquisitely through every nerve in my body, shaking me to the core.

Andre sat back in the sand then, his face wet with my juices, and I dropped on weak knees beside him, catching my breath. Celia took the opportunity to strip, baring her stunning beauty. Her nude figure in the moonlight was an awesome sight. Kneeling beside her husband, she went to work with eager fingers and quickly pulled Andre's erection out of his pants. His thick cock sprouted from a dark patch of pubic hair, whereas Celia had almost no hair at all down there.

While I watched, Celia lowered her mouth over the bulbous crown and began sucking Andre's fat dick with a voraciousness that rekindled my own passion. Andre glanced up from Celia's hungry antics to meet my eyes, and I know he saw the same intensity in my face, the same fire in my eyes, that he felt in his wife's attention between his legs. Perhaps it was my rapacious stare that tripped him, or Celia's hot, wet mouth swallowing his cock, but suddenly Andre was coming. His wife pulled her mouth away, and his prick spouted white cream like a volcano as he dug his fingers deep into the sand. Celia licked most of the semen off his penis and stomach. I couldn't resist coming over for a taste, choosing a drop that had landed on Celia's cheek for my sample. She smiled when I licked the salty fluid off her skin.

Andre lay back on the sand as he caught his breath. Celia and I hurriedly removed his clothes. "Here," she said to me, taking hold of her husband's semi-hard penis and aiming it straight up. Her implication was clear. With a greedy grin of my own, I crawled to Andre's side and quickly straddled him. Celia held his cock at my slit, and I screwed myself down on it all the way until my butt came to rest against his balls. I felt his prick swell inside me, regaining its maximum length and stiffness. It was really a colossal dick, and the way it filled me up, expanding my channel, was unforgettable.

At the same time, Celia swung a thigh over Andre's head and, facing me, she seated herself upon his mouth. He reached around her torso to fill his hands with her breasts. She sighed happily and began grinding her cunt against his lips while he snacked on her sex. Celia's molten eyes met mine as I started to fuck Andre. She watched me lift and lower my body, my movements sensually casual at first, then more ardent. Returning her lusty stare, I began to hump Andre more aggressively, slamming down on his dick. My occupational instincts took over, and I started rotating my hips as only an expert hula girl can. Andre responded with a moan of delight. He lifted his hips off the sand, driving his cock deeper into my pussy. The ti leaves of my hula skirt rustled seductively with every move I made. Celia was whimpering and rocking herself atop Andre's tongue, her eyes slitted with passion. We stroked and fondled each other's heaving breasts and kissed a little, too. It was the perfect threeway, fulfilling my carnal needs perfectly. All the while, the Pacific crashed ashore some twenty-five yards off and the tropical wind whistled through the coconut palms over our heads.

Celia and I continued riding Andre's tongue and penis and playing with each other until all the myriad sensations overpowered me. Momentarily lost in my second climax of the night, I rocked to and fro on Andre's pole while Celia embraced me. She peaked at nearly the same time, brought to a violent orgasm by Andre's expert tongue. When she finally dismounted his face, I saw that Andre's chin was drenched with her slick honey. That's when I felt Andre's cock erupt inside me, blasting come deep in my sex. He bellowed something in his native tongue and held my hips tightly until his climax passed.

We should have been exhausted, but instead of sleeping we spent the few remaining hours before sunrise talking, laughing and listening to the waves. At dawn, early enough that no one was around to see us, we swam naked in the warm ocean. Then we dressed and went to find breakfast, after which I gave my new friends a local's tour of the island. They were game for anything—parasailing, snorkeling, even a ride on the famous Sugar Cane Train. By early afternoon, the lack of sleep caught up with us. We went back to my place for showers and a snooze on my outdoor lanai. In Hawaii, where the weather is perfect almost all the time, we spend a lot of time on our lanais and furnish them accordingly. Celia stretched out on one of the two cushioned chaise recliners; I took the other. Andre crashed on the couch. Overhead the sky was robin's-egg blue, but I knew it wouldn't be for long. Where I live, we get a little afternoon rain almost every day.

Sure enough, I was awakened a few hours later by the kiss of raindrops on my face. The air was still, the drops infrequent. I opened my eyes and smiled at the sky. The blue spaces were rapidly diminishing as small clouds merged into larger ones. The largest hung right overhead, a dark mass fringed in wispy white and shaped, believe it or not, like the torso of an exceptionally curvaceous woman.

As the gentle afternoon shower continued, I turned and found Celia watching me from where she lay. She looked so desirable with her dark hair mussed, her lips full and pouty, and her face flecked with raindrops. Our eyes met, and I saw the want there, the hunger. A twinge of excitement shot through me, and I motioned Celia over. She came quickly, bending to me for a sensual kiss. I opened my arms for her, and she lay down atop me. We kissed and snuggled for a minute or two before the urge to feel each other, skin to skin, became too strong to resist. When we had arrived at my place earlier that day, I had loaned Celia some casual clothes to lounge around in after showering. I knew the brief cotton shorts and loose tank top would slip off very easily, and Celia proved it for me, sliding the shorts down her legs and the top over her head in about two seconds flat. Giggling, I pulled off my T-shirt and shorts, and then Celia and I helped each other out of our bras and panties. I had barely a moment to take in the incredible sexiness of her body before she sealed herself to me. The rain caressed our bare skin while our hands went everywhere. Our legs rubbed and our cunts kissed. I could literally feel the brush of her tiny pubic patch against my own vulva and the wetness of her sex upon my labia as our juices mingled.

"Turn around. I want to taste you," I entreated Celia. I hadn't touched her pussy before, nor even seen it up close, and I desperately wanted to. She grinned and did as I asked, realigning herself with her head between my legs and her pubic region right over my face. Her thighs on either side of my head were smooth and warm. My own inner thighs registered the touch of Celia's ticklishly soft hair as she pressed her face to my slit. It was so different, so thrilling to have a woman down there, lapping at my slit. I wanted Andre in the action, too, and that made me look over to the couch to see if he had awakened.

Andre was not only wide-awake, he was watching us with his cock out and his hand around the shaft. Our eyes met, and he grinned wolfishly. I could tell he was drawing out the anticipation for a minute or two while enjoying the show, but he wouldn't be able to resist much longer. His hungry stare enflamed my lust. Turning my undivided attention back to Celia's pretty cunt, I licked between her swollen nether lips with newfound zeal. When I zoned in on her clitoris she exclaimed, "Oh god, yes, that's it!" and lowered her hips another inch to really plaster her sweet pussy against my mouth.

Andre muttered something I couldn't make out—the words were garbled with passion—and pulled off his pants and underwear. Then he stepped over to us with his huge, throbbing dick leading the way. Straddling the lounge, he stood over me with his balls just a few inches above my face and prepared to nudge the head of his erection between Celia's slippery folds. My eyes widened at the close-up view of his bulbous crown. I saw a drop of precome glistening at the tip; then it was lost from view as he penetrated her. Celia gasped against my sex when she felt Andre's heavy prick slide home. I kept licking, my tongue flicking across not just a juicy pussy but a thick cock as well. It was easy to lap at Andre's heavy ball sac, too. Andre pulled out halfway; Celia squirmed her hips impatiently until her husband slammed into her again, eliciting more cries of delight from both Celia and me. All the while she kept busy between my legs, flicking her tongue across my swollen clitoris and pumping her fingers into my vagina. It was a sensory blitz that threatened to unravel me from the inside out.

Andre grabbed Celia's supple hips and began pumping hard and fast into her. His prick was a blur; his balls bounced wildly. Placing my fingers on either side of his cock, I splayed Celia's folds wide, then resumed slathering her inner pink recesses—as well as Andre's hammering dick—with my saliva. They both moaned with pleasure and fucked harder still, making the chaise creak ominously. The rain, fragrant and warm, continued to fall, and by now we were all thoroughly doused, which only added to the thrill of our lovemaking. "Oh, I'm going to come!" Celia shouted, her voice smothered by my pulsing cunt.

"Come on then, let's come together," Andre cried through clenched teeth as he vigorously fucked Celia. "Kai, come with us!"

I almost did, but in the end it was even better the way it happened, since I still had my senses when both of them came unglued. I have to give Celia credit; somehow she kept her tongue buried in my pussy throughout the gargantuan climax that ripped through her moments later. She held on to my thighs and worked my clit relentlessly until I felt my own orgasmic storm gather on the horizon.

With a cry like a wild animal, Andre rammed into Celia once more and cut loose. His hips bucked against her ass as his cock, buried deep within her syrupy depths, spurted its load. Excitedly, I kept licking their sloppy juncture, hoping for a taste of Andre's come. After a bit he pulled out of his wife's sticky hole, and several drops of his semen rained down on my tongue and face. It was so salacious that I came at once, my body wracked by wave after wave of orgasmic bliss. Celia's ministrations between my legs kept it going, leaving me insensate for a full minute. She was in no hurry to give up suckling my sensitive clit. Andre staggered back, spent, and watched us until Celia and I had both had enough.

The following afternoon, I parted company with Celia and Andre. They took a red-eye flight back home, and I donned my hula-girl costume for another luau performance, confident in the knowledge that my threesome pursuits were only just beginning.

Dreaming of Julia

CELESTE STONE

"Oh, Julia," Aaron whispered. "I'm going to fuck the living daylights out of you."

His strong hand worked between my legs as he spoke, his fingertips first stroking the trembling muscles of my inner thighs, before he placed his palm directly over the front of my pale-blue panties. When Aaron spoke again, he let me know that he could feel my arousal even through the silk.

"Julia, baby, you're so fucking wet."

Each time he spoke, I felt myself respond. I actually thought that he might make me come with only the combination of the slow circles of his fingers on my panties and his soft crooning words. The melding of the two was almost overwhelming.

"Are you ready for me to bend you over the bed and lift your skirt? To pull your undies down and drive my cock home? Are you ready, Julia?" His fingers slid beneath my panties, slipping sweetly between the swollen lips of my pussy. I groaned and arched against him, showing him with my body exactly what I wanted him to do—which was this: go deeper. His fingers followed my silent command, first one and then two driving inside me, overlapping, twisting and filling me.

"Tell me," he insisted. "Tell me what you want, Julia."

I wanted him to keep touching my pussy. But more than that, I wanted him to keep calling me "Julia."

Because, you see, my name's Celeste.

"Come on, baby," he said, his mouth against my neck. "Tell me."

I swallowed hard. I knew he was waiting. He'd given me the introduction, and he wanted me to play the part, to play the role of sultry, dark-haired Julia, with the high cheekbones and the large hazel eyes. Julia was the girl who had recently come to work at my law firm as our receptionist. A girl Aaron had no idea I'd met before—more than met—someone I had the most decadent memories of sleeping with, rolling over and over on the bed, my mouth to her neck, to her flat belly, to her pussy.

But that moment wasn't the time to get into that sort of ancient history. It was the time to draw upon my neophyte thespian skills and actually be Julia.

"Oh yes," I told Aaron. "Bend me over and fuck me."

"Whatever you say, Julia." I could hear the smile in his voice and feel how hard this whole playacting exercise had made him when he did just as he'd promised. He bent me over our king-size mattress, lifted my flirty little skirt and pulled down my panties. When Aaron only half undresses me, I almost come from that sensation alone. The sexiness of being partially dressed turned me on, and when he let me feel his cock, so hard, so ready, I had to groan.

He gripped my hips and then waited, making me beg wordlessly for him to continue. Making me speak gibberish—speak in tongues—in an effort to make him give me what I so desperately craved. I felt for a fact how turned on I was. Although I always get good and creamy for Aaron, the amount of wetness this time was surprising even to me. Was that because I was being Julia?

Maybe. Because as he finally gave in and started to fuck me—slipping the head of his rod between my nether lips and thrusting one time hard, right from the start, to coat his cock with my juices—I have to admit my mind wandered. To the time I'd met Julia before.

Our illicit encounter had taken place nearly ten years prior to this at a sorority party, when we'd ended up in the same bed together. The guy we'd both been flirting with all night had fallen asleep between us, and we had wound up making love to each other. Since that night, my mind had occasionally wandered back to that event, and when it did, I longed to fulfill our unrequited three-way fantasy, nearly as much as I longed to kiss her again. Unfortunately, Julia hadn't gone to my school—she'd been in town visiting a friend—and I hadn't seen her again until she was hired at the law office where I work as a paralegal.

"God, Julia," Aaron hissed. "Do you always get this wet right from the start?"

He was playing as if this were our first time, rather than three years into a decadent relationship. And although we'd done that sharing thing couples do as they get to know each other, he had no reason to guess that the woman he'd seen at the front desk was the same one to whom I'd lost my girl-cherry.

Now, I was gushing, my juices dampening the tops of my thighs, the *slip-slap* sound of his cock driving into me an added bonus to all the fantasy foreplay. Yeah, I get wet for Aaron. But the risqué game we were playing that night made me wetter than normal. He thrust inside me again, and I felt myself contract around him, as if trying to hold him inside me, to keep him there, filling me.

The thought of him fucking Julia was not only turning me on, it was also turning something else on inside me.

What was the emotion I was feeling?

Not jealousy—no. But something I'd read about online: *comp-ersion*, getting an erotic charge when your partner is with another person. Yet I didn't want him to be with that other person alone. I wanted to be right there with him, and oh, did that image of the three of us excite me.

Aaron gripped my short blonde hair, and I wondered if he was imagining the dark, shoulder-length mane of Julia's hair. I wondered if he was pretending my blue eyes were her brownish-green ones. And I wondered if he saw her full ass instead of my tight bottom.

When I turned to look at him over my shoulder, when I saw the intensity on his face, I had to think that he did. He was lost in that middle ground, where he was fucking me, but seeing her. Fucking her in his mind, while touching me. That overlap of imagination and reality was taking him to a brand-new level of pleasure—and I was caught in the same place, being fucked by him while being her. And, god, I loved every second.

Aaron slid one hand beneath my body, pressed his thumb

against my clit, and I began to grind on him, to push forward with my slim hips so that I could feel both the pressure I needed from below and the fullness I craved deep inside. I lost myself in the sensations as I pictured Julia sharing this exquisite moment with us.

"Oh my fucking god," I said, the words a whisper, a murmur, a prayer. He continued banging me so hard our whole bed groaned with the intensity of his movements, and the power behind his thrusts made my legs shake.

"I'm going to come," I whispered, and Aaron's voice grew soft.

"Oh, Julia," he moaned as he came.

"Oh, Julia?" I trilled the next day, when I walked by the reception desk—I could almost hear Aaron saying her name as I spoke. "Can I have a word?" My heart was racing at the thought of what I was about to do and what I was going to suggest, but I couldn't stop myself. The idea had formed in the night, and I'd been up into the wee hours, planning while Aaron slept.

What had started out as a fun bit of foreplay—*I'm going to fuck you and call you Julia*—had solidified into an X-rated plan. I'd turned the thought around and around in my mind. And although I didn't ask Aaron first how he would feel, somehow I felt secure enough that Aaron would be more than pleased with what I had in mind for the three of us.

How had my man even known about Julia in the first place? The answer was simple. He'd seen her when he'd picked me up for lunch. With his dirty mind, there had been no hesitation before he brought her into our bed in spirit. I wondered what he would do when I brought her into bed for real, because now I only needed Julia's agreement to turn our fantasy into reality. I say "only" as if I was already sure she'd agree. But if she were at all the same type of girl she'd been a decade before, then there would be no question. I had often thought back to that one night together, the way she'd gripped my shoulders as I'd licked her pussy. The way she'd let me make her come once, twice, three times, so that she was breathless, panting, shaking all over. I wanted to share all of that sensuality with Aaron.

Had she thought about that crazy evening over the years? When she was alone in bed, or even with a lover, had she closed her eyes and called forth those sultry memories? I hoped so. But more than that, I hoped that she'd even remember who I was.

Would she gaze at me and recall the way I looked back then—my short hair dyed blue, my eyeliner raccoon heavy? Would she be able to see beyond my exterior as a proper paralegal, in my beige pencil skirt and neat white blouse, to recognize the beating of my dirty heart?

I felt my cheeks flush with nervous excitement, and I forced myself not to hold my breath after reintroducing myself. To my relief, when I told her who I was, she grinned back at me. "I know," she said. "I've never forgotten that night."

Seeing the memory light up her eyes, I felt myself getting wet once more.

We went to lunch together, and I laid out my plans. "What do you think?" I asked, after I explained the scenario. "A little tease for my beau."

"Kiss me to seal the deal." She grinned.

"Wait until Friday night," I countered, although I had no idea how *I* would wait. I wanted to go to the ladies' room right then, to take care of the building need inside me. I wanted to drag her after me, press her up against the tiled wall, kiss her until my lips were bruised, until she begged me for mercy. But even more than that, I wanted Aaron to be there when I did.

The night before, Aaron had pretended I was Julia. Come Friday evening, there would be no pretending.

To my delight, she arrived right on time—a half hour before I expected my man to come home. When she saw me, she wolf-whistled.

"You look good as a brunette," Julia exclaimed, walking around me and checking out my look. I'd snagged a wig that was as close to her hair color and style as I could find. In semidarkness, I thought I looked quite similar to her.

"You'll wait here," I told her, showing her our bedroom. "We're going to blow his mind."

"As well as other parts of his anatomy," Julia teased.

Oh, was Aaron ever in for a sweet surprise. Julia started to undress as soon as we were in the room. She said, "Ever since you mentioned the concept to me, I've been going out of my head. I swear, I've come more times during the past few days than I have in the past six months." Just like the Julia I remembered. The one who couldn't get enough. "Do you think it would be bad if I make myself come one time before he gets here?"

I sucked in my breath, looking at her breasts and the strip of dark curls over her pussy.

"No," I managed not to stutter. "I don't think that would be a problem. I mean, if I can watch." But right then, I heard a key in the front door.

"Wait here," I told her, hurrying as fast as I could in my spiked shoes. The *click-clack* of the heels on the hardwood floor alerted Aaron right away that something was up. Generally, the first thing I do when

I get home is take *off* my high heels, not put on a taller pair. He stood in the foyer, watching me approach him, and he gave a low chuckle when I stepped into his arms.

"Julia," he smiled, "so nice to see you again."

You have no idea how nice, I thought, but didn't say. Instead, I dropped to my knees and worked the fly on his slacks. I was hungry for him—truly ravenous. I hoped he was as ready for me. I needn't have worried, though. Aaron's *always* ready. His cock sprang out when I set him free, and I let him enjoy a few moments of powerful sucking before I stood once more.

"Don't stop," he urged, his tone holding a note of begging.

"Let's bring it to the bedroom," I cooed, unable to wait another minute. I walked at a fast clip to the bedroom, not daring to look back, but I heard him following me. I made it into the room before him, and then pressed myself back against the wall. As soon as he entered the room, he sucked in his breath. I'd lit candles, and they glowed everywhere, providing just enough light to see the naked woman on the bed. Aaron had been far enough behind me that he simply assumed the woman was me. That is, until he got close enough to the mattress.

"Celeste," he stammered, and I stepped away from the wall, where I'd stood in shadow.

"You mean Julia," I corrected him.

"I mean," he said. "I mean," he tried again. Then finally, "I don't know what I mean." His voice was a whisper. I could tell from the look on his face that he thought he'd walked into a dream. As if he said or did the wrong thing, the dream would disappear, and he'd find himself in bed alone with his hand on his dick.

"That's fine," Julia said. "Just leave everything to us."

The last time Julia and I had been together, the boy who we'd both been flirting with had been asleep. This time, the two of us had a male figure to focus our attention on. But that didn't mean we didn't play with each other. First, Julia kissed Aaron, and then she motioned for me to join her on the bed. While my man watched, Julia stroked her fingertips over my cheekbones, then gripped my shoulders and brought me in for a kiss. Aaron sighed, stunned by the vision. I could guess what we looked like: two pretty brunettes, making out for his viewing pleasure. But it wasn't simply for his viewing pleasure—because kissing Julia turned me on even more than "being" Julia had.

I let her lead, felt her mouth on mine, felt her lips slip from my own as she moved to my throat, kissing here, licking there. Then she was sliding the spaghetti straps of my chemise off my shoulders to reveal my pert breasts. Julia's breasts are full and heavy, more than handfuls. Mine are small and perky, and when she just barely rubbed her palm over my nipples, they stood out firm and hard.

Her touch flickered through my whole body. She'd only kissed me, barely stroked me, and yet if I'd been a man, I would have been sporting a rock-hard erection, like I imagined Aaron was. As a girl, my panties were damp—an ocean of sex juices between my legs. Julia seemed to guess that. She pushed me back on the bed, hiked up my satiny slip and brought her mouth to the split between my thighs. Then she quickly, forcefully lapped at me through my panties.

This time, Aaron didn't simply suck in his breath. He gasped. It was almost as if he could feel her mouth on him, simultaneously. Was he living vicariously through his two Julias? I didn't want to leave him out. I nodded my head toward him, and Julia understood my intention. She reached her hand out and grabbed his, pulling him toward the bed.

Aaron shed his clothes in a heartbeat and then joined us. Julia made space for him, as if she were the hostess, as if this were her boudoir instead of ours. She shifted, let him settle and then began to take turns, first licking me through my panties, then letting her mouth bob on Aaron's cock.

I thought he was going to pass out from an overload of pleasure. The look on his face was so sublime—different from the beginning. Not as if he couldn't believe his luck, but as if he had arrived in the living fantasy of his dreams.

But as good as Julia's mouth felt on my cunt, I couldn't simply lie back and enjoy the pleasure. I wanted to be part of the action. Julia seemed to understand my goal as I gently moved her aside and worked my mouth down the length of my man's rod.

"Shut your eyes," I instructed, and Aaron did. What a good boy!

I sucked him hard, before slipping my tongue around the head of his cock. Then I sat back on my heels and watched as Julia mimicked my actions.

I watched the blissful expression on Aaron's face. He didn't move, didn't push up his hips, didn't instruct us or beg us. He simply let us take turns, licking his cock, and then kissing his balls. I knew he could feel Julia's rich dark hair against his skin, and then my own faux tresses brushing him. Back and forth we went, until I saw the change in my man. The expression on his face told me that he was moments away from climax.

At this time, I took charge. I nudged Julia away and climbed astride my boyfriend. I was not ready to share this most private experience with her—at least not yet. The responsibility of actually making Aaron come belonged to me. But Julia didn't mind in the slightest. She turned her attention to me, cradling my head in her hands as she kissed me, feeling my body tremble as I rode Aaron's cock up and down, cowgirl style.

I thought of the time Julia and I had been lovers—ten years ago, but really only a blink. I thought of the way she'd looked as she came, her eyes so huge and dark. Her full bottom lip bitten into by her teeth. The way she'd let herself go upon climaxing had unleashed something in me, as if her freedom had given me permission to truly experience undiluted pleasure for the first time.

And here she was, unlocking something in me once more. As she kissed me, she pulled the wig off my head, turning me back into me. Now there was only one Julia in the room. One Julia, one Celeste and one Aaron; three bodies connected, overlapping, working together. She kissed me harder, and I slid one hand down her body and found the nub of her clit, rubbing her with my thumb even as the pressure built inside me.

"I'm going to—" Aaron said, but Julia finished the statement for each of them, saying, "Celeste, I'm going to come."

"Do it," I hissed, talking to both at once, feeling Julia crest to orgasm on my fingertips as Aaron lifted me up with the power of his climax. A shudder worked through my own body. I felt responsible for both of my lovers' satisfaction, and then my turn arrived. I ground my body against Aaron's, threw back my head and came.

No longer was the memory of being with Julia the most exciting time in my life. We had surpassed that magical evening and—with Aaron's help—had created one that was even more special.

Ski-Lodge Lust

DOUG SOLOMON

When I first laid eyes on Lila and Jeri, I knew they had never worn skis before. Slipping, sliding and flailing for balance, they inched their way up the gentle slope toward me. Trying to teach these two how to ski in one hour would be an impossible task, I thought irritably. But I didn't know that behind the goggles and the bulky, figure-concealing ski suits were two of the most gorgeous, oversexed young women I would ever meet. I would soon thank my lucky stars that Jeri and Lila had signed up for a private lesson with me.

The two women were practically in hysterics over their struggles, so I knew they weren't taking themselves too seriously. Watching them, my chagrin faded, and I couldn't help laughing. I waved and beckoned to them encouragingly, which drew a pair of pretty smiles.

The shorter one half turned to the other, and though she kept her voice low, the movement of her lips confirmed what she said: "Ooh, he's hot."

I must've reacted in some way, because they both started—and promptly lost their balance, spilling headlong into the snow with arms and legs akimbo. I hastened over to help them both up.

"Thanks," said the one who'd spoken before. She swept her lustrous brown hair out of her face while her blonde companion clung to my shoulder.

"Are you Lila and Jeri, by any chance?" I asked.

The brunette nodded. Her cheeks were pink—from the cold or from embarrassment, I didn't know. "I'm Lila," she replied, breaking into a nervous grin as she wobbled precariously on her skis. Nodding toward her taller companion, she added, "She's Jeri."

I shook their gloved hands. "Nice to meet you. I'm Doug, your instructor."

"Lucky us," said Jeri, her smile and tone blatantly flirtatious. Lila giggled and elbowed her friend in the side. Their goggles hid their eyes, but I could tell they were both looking me over from head to foot. It's true that my ski outfit was considerably more streamlined than theirs, but with the way they were checking me out, I almost felt naked.

I cleared my throat. "I'm guessing that you two have never been on skis before now?"

Jeri burst out laughing. "Whatever gave you that idea?" She had a small, perfect nose, full red lips and snow-white teeth, but other than those details I had no real sense of what she or her companion looked like.

"That's all right, you'll pick it up quickly," I said. "First thing to learn is how to fall…"

For the next hour, under dark skies that promised more snow, we went over the basics. After her third or fourth tumble, Jeri explained that she and Lila were city girls who usually avoided cold-weather places. For a lark, they had decided to spend a weekend away from their usual stomping grounds and do something totally different. Unlike them, I grew up with tilted horizons and snow on the ground from October to May. I was practically born on a pair of skis.

Still, what Lila and Jeri lacked in experience they made up for in pluck as they gamely tried every skiing technique I showed them. They both exhibited some natural athleticism, too. When I pointed this out, they admitted they had been on their college swim team a few years back. "Jeri's favorite outfit is a swimsuit," Lila said.

I imagined Jeri in a hot bikini, with physical attributes that would prove remarkably accurate later: long, supple legs, sizeable breasts and a nice, tight ass.

"Lila's the one with all the school records," was Jeri's rejoinder.

The vision in my mind suddenly included Lila, too; I imagined the smaller woman in a spandex racing suit that stretched beautifully over her smooth curves as her lithe body knifed through the water of a swimming pool.

"Doug? Is this right?" Jeri was attempting to stop her forward motion on the snow by inverting her skis. Just as I came up alongside her, her skis crossed and she toppled right into my arms, sending us both into the snow. I was pretty sure she'd done it on purpose. My cock was coming to life fast. Over Jeri's shoulder, I saw Lila peering down at us, a bemused expression on her face. As she extended a hand to Jeri, she pushed her sunglasses up to her forehead, showing me her beautiful emerald-green eyes for the first time. I saw a mischievous, flirty twinkle in them.

In the process of extricating herself, Jeri's thigh pressed against my groin. Despite her heavy clothing, I knew she felt my swollen hard-on. "Thanks for breaking my fall," she said coquettishly.

Somehow we got through the rest of the lesson, but not without a great deal of physical contact. They were definitely interested in more than just ski lessons from me.

"Are you free later?" Jeri asked as I led her and Lila back toward the lodge.

"Sure," I said. "I get off at four."

"Have a drink with us at the bar. Around five?"

"Sure," I said again, and we parted ways.

At four o'clock I went back to my place, showered and changed clothes. Returning to the resort, I let myself in through the restaurant kitchen and peeked through the door into the bar—and my jaw dropped.

Lila and Jeri sat at the bar with drinks in hand, waiting for me. They were in their mid-twenties and gorgeous. Lila wore a snug black sweater and tight blue jeans, accentuating every curve of her slender frame. Jeri had on a red top that clung to her full, perky breasts, while her skirt and boots drew attention to her long, sexy legs. I gave them each a hug and a kiss and dropped onto the stool between them, the envy of every guy in the place.

We chatted and sipped drinks. Almost from the start, it was crystal clear where the evening was going. When the carnal vibes became too powerful to resist any longer, Lila and Jeri exchanged a meaningful look, then turned to me. "Would you like to come up to our room?" Jeri asked.

My cock grew as stiff as a flagpole. I paid for the drinks and slid off my stool. "After you two."

Their room, like the rest of the lodge, was dark and cozy, with rustic wood furnishings and a faux animal rug on the floor. Outside the window, big snowflakes were falling. Lila hung the Do NOT DISTURB sign on the door handle, then I heard the lock click.

Jeri stepped into my arms. I bent to kiss her, and she responded hungrily, seeking my tongue with hers. I felt Lila join our embrace on my left, so I turned to kiss her, too. She reciprocated with all the pent-up desire that Jeri had shown, if not more. While Lila's soft lips were pressed to mine, Jeri lifted her own shirt over her head and then unhooked her bra, which she let drop to the floor. I turned back to her, cupping her breasts in my hands as our tongues twirled together. I slid my hands down to her waist, encountered her skirt and went to work on the buttons in front. She shimmied out of the skirt and pressed herself against me once more. My hands closed on her ass, which was naked except for the thin cotton thong running between those succulent globes.

Lila, who was still nuzzling my neck, unbuttoned my pants and reached in to fondle my rock-hard prick. She had already taken off her sweater; her breasts were full and ripe and crowned by small, pink nipples that flushed and stiffened when I took them between my fingers.

"Sit down, Doug," said Jeri. I sat on the edge of the bed and the two women quickly pulled off my boots, pants and underwear. I had barely gotten my shirt off before Jeri grabbed hold of my dick and started sucking it with gusto. She left room for Lila, who joined her friend between my knees and gave my balls a sensual tongue bath. Jeri moaned feverishly as she slurped up and down my pole. Lila sucked my balls into her mouth and slid her tongue down my perineum. When she rimmed my asshole, I almost came unglued.

Then Jeri stood up, kicked off her boots and squirmed out of her thong, exposing her dewy pussy lips and a minuscule triangle of golden pubic hair. With an eager grin, she pushed me flat on the bed and straddled my face. Her knees were on either side of my head, and her smooth thighs blocked my peripheral vision, channeling my line of sight straight up her hard body. Lila promptly took my dick into her hungry mouth while Jeri lowered herself until her damp vulva sat against my lips.

"Eat me, Doug," Jeri demanded. "Suck my clit!" It was a nice plump button, plainly visible and waiting for attention. I darted my tongue out and explored Jeri's folds first, making her wait for the more intense feelings she craved. She had a delicious cunt, and it began to drip honey as I slid my tongue in and out of her. Jeri wriggled madly atop me, enjoying the sensations but yearning for more. Desperately, she rubbed her hot spot against my chin. Relenting at last, I zeroed in on her clit. At the first touch of my tongue there, Jeri grunted and rocked her hips forward, pushing her sensitive button farther into my mouth. Wrapping my lips around that pulsing point, I soon had Jeri panting and yelping like a wild animal.

All the while, Lila bobbed up and down on my cock with her mouth and made salacious noises of her own. Her technique was so good that I was dismayed when, a minute or two later, she suddenly stopped. My excitement flared anew when I felt the touch of her hand on my penis as she aimed the shaft straight up. The next moment I felt the warm, velvety clutch of her cunt envelop my shaft as Lila impaled herself. I could feel her opening up inside, parting wetly for my rod. Lila's ass finally settled against my thighs, and then she began to fuck me, lifting her nubile body to the top of my prick and then lowering herself to the base with ever-increasing speed. She rode me vigorously for several minutes, making the bed squeak and groan, while Jeri continued to ride my tongue with escalating lust.

Eventually, Lila slammed down against my root and stayed there, gyrating her hips like a belly dancer as she gave in to a monstrous orgasm and exclaimed, "I'm coming! I'm coming!" Lila's cries of ecstasy ratcheted up Jeri's excitement to the breaking point until she, too, reached her peak, arching her back and squeezing her breasts while she crushed her clit against my mouth. Her thighs squeezed my face as her juices drenched my lips and chin.

Jeri and Lila's powerful climaxes worked their magic on me. I felt a jolt within my balls, and two seconds later my cock started pumping hot cream deep into Lila's sex. She was still shaking atop me, her frame wracked by the throes of an orgasm that was now extended by my own explosion within her depths. When she finally climbed off me, my erection smacked against my belly, ready to go another round. I wasn't so sure about my companions, but that just shows how little I knew Jeri and Lila. Jeri took one look at my unflagging tumescence and promptly took her friend's place, screwing herself down on my shaft all the way to my balls. Her channel felt smaller and tighter around my hefty cock than Lila's had, but her dripping juices made penetration easy. Jeri was determined to draw out another orgasm for both of us.

As for Lila, she looked on intently for a minute, catching her breath. But when Jeri started bouncing zealously up and down on my cock, Lila couldn't resist getting back in the action. She shot me a wicked grin and quickly assumed Jeri's former place aboard my face. I've always had a lot of stamina, but these two feisty women intended to test my limits. I was more than happy to go along with the experiment!

Squatting on her haunches over my mouth, Lila chose to face away from me, toward my feet—or in this case, toward Jeri. Before she settled into position I had a quick glimpse of her pubic mound, which was just a tiny landing strip the color of dark chocolate. The skin all around it was smooth and milky-white. Mostly, my view was of Lila's perfect asscheeks, her tiny rear hole and the delicate lips of her pussy. Her dripping slit had a different taste than Jeri's, but it was equally intoxicating. I licked up and down her whole cunt, which made her jerk and thrash violently. It was easy to snake my tongue up through the well-spread crack of her ass to her anus, just as she had done to me. Immediately, I discovered that was an extremely erotic spot for Lila, who came again within seconds. She tossed her head back and forth and practically broke down with sobs of joy. Jeri hugged her friend close while she powered herself up and down on my cock for another few minutes, but then she, too, could take no more. I felt her cunt convulse around my shaft, and she let loose a fresh stream of warm fluids. When her senses cleared, she correctly sensed that my own climax was imminent. "I want to taste your come," she cried, climbing off my penis just as it began to shoot semen into the air. I uttered a guttural cry as I felt my balls drain completely. In a matter of seconds, there was come everywhere: on the girls' faces, on their breasts, on my stomach. Jeri and Lila licked it up wherever it fell. Finally they both collapsed onto the bed, exhausted.

The light from the window had grown dim. After a while,

when I thought my companions were asleep, I got dressed and headed for the door.

"Doug, could we have another private lesson tomorrow?" Lila was up on one elbow, looking at me with big, shining eyes.

"Sure," I replied. "It's my day off. Let's try cross-country skiing. I think you guys will like it better than downhill."

"You're the expert," Lila said, returning my smile.

"Meet me at the rental shop around noon." I gave her a little wave and slipped out.

The next day they showed up right on time. I was glad to see them—and so was my cock, which stirred in my pants at the memory of the previous evening's workout. Jeri and Lila greeted me with two passionate kisses. I think people going by were a little shocked, but I didn't care; it meant this day had a good chance of ending up like yesterday had. The weather was much different, however. The storm had passed, the sky was blue, and the temperature was rising. A brand-new blanket of snow covered everything.

"Let's get you some cross-country skis," I said. After Lila and Jeri were properly outfitted, I led them away from the resort along an easy, sublime route through the woods. The entire forest sparkled with melting icicles. I let the women set our pace; they seemed much more comfortable on their skis that day, and we made good time. In a few minutes we crossed the resort property boundary, and a few minutes after that we came upon a small cabin in a clearing.

"Look at that place. It's so cute!" Jeri exclaimed.

"Want to go inside?" I asked.

"Sure!" Lila said. "But how?"

"It's mine. Nothing fancy, but it's home. Come on."

We took off our skis and boots on the front stoop and went inside, padding around in our socks. The grand tour took all of two minutes, considering there's only one bedroom, one bathroom and a small kitchen. My favorite spot is the back porch, which I had screened in a few years back so I could sleep out there in the summer. I'd installed a small bed and a wood stove, too, which let me use the porch in colder months. We ended up in there, so I busied myself lighting some logs. When I turned around, Lila and Jeri were sitting on my bed, undressing each other. My dick got hard so fast that it was almost painful. They chortled at my surprised expression and continued undressing. Once all their clothes were piled up on the floor, they sat hip to hip at the edge of the bed and held out their hands to me. For a second I paused, admiring their beautiful feminine nudity. They were both so ripe and ready for action, however, that to wait another millisecond would have been a crime. I went and stood before them, and they helped me get naked. The stove hadn't warmed the room appreciably yet, but I found the cold air bracing. It turned the girls' nipples hard and rosy colored; they looked quite striking atop the ivory-white mounds of their breasts. With a wolfish grin, Lila fell to sucking on my cock, while Jeri grasped the base of my manhood and stroked the lower half in her pulsing grip. I wanted to take charge this time, though, so after a minute I extended my arms around their shoulders and pulled them down onto the mattress with me. Surprised, they whooped and laughed, but their laughter turned to moans and sighs of pleasure as the three of us slid and rolled together. Unaccustomed to the weight, my old bed protested, but I barely noticed. Lying sandwiched between Lila and Jeri's soft, undulating bodies was a little slice of heaven itself.

Eventually I sat up, took hold of Jeri's hips and pulled her toward my erection. "Yeah, Doug," she breathed, getting onto her hands and knees and waggling her round rump at me. "Take me from behind." The petals of her sex, shiny with her natural lube, peeked out below the crack of her ass. Eagerly, I pushed the head of my cock between her plump labia and slid in. My length and thickness made her gasp with delight and sparked a shudder that passed through her agile frame. Then she started to move, rocking back and forth on all fours against my thrusts. Lila stroked her hair and back, watching with wide eyes.

"That's it, that's it," Jeri said, her voice rough with lust. "He's fucking me good, Lila." Impulsively, she gave her friend a kiss on the lips. I saw a look of surprise pass between them. They kissed again, more fervently this time. Lila reached out and petted Jeri's breasts with hands that were less tentative by the second. Jeri mewled and lowered her head into Lila's lap. I saw her thrust out her tongue to taste Lila's cunt. They hadn't touched intimately the day before, and I gathered this was uncharted territory for them. Caught up in the passion of the moment, and with Lila's ripe sex right there in front of her face, so pretty and inviting, who could blame Jeri for trying something new? Certainly not Lila, who opened her thighs to give her friend better access. I saw such a look of raw animal lust on Lila's face that my own ardor shot up several notches. I palmed the globes of Jeri's ass and drove my cock into her with frenetic energy. Her shouts rose in pitch until finally she bellowed into Lila's crotch, "I'm coming!" Her vagina contracted and sent a torrent of slick fluids down my prick.

Lila's moans were also getting louder as Jeri continued her oral exploration of her friend's juicy slit. I was still pumping away at Jeri's cunt when Lila shuddered and grabbed up fistfuls of Jeri's hair. Her eyes closed, and she turned inward for a moment, relishing a quick, sharp climax. At last Jeri raised her head and the two women kissed again, sharing the taste of Lila's sweet sex. When Jeri rolled off to the side, though, Lila proved she still needed deeper and stronger sensations. "My turn!" she cried, lying flat on the bed and spreading her knees for me. I mounted her missionary style and began pumping my hips between her thighs as my desperate cock probed the depths of her pussy. Her body felt so luscious and warm beneath me that in mere seconds I was slamming ferociously into her. She urged me on, curving her hands around my buttocks and pulling them apart as she screamed with pleasure. Jeri came around and, finding my anus nicely exposed by Lila's gripping hands, she pressed her thumb into my tight orifice. The sensation of Jeri's thumb lodged fully in my asshole, along with the velvety paradise of Lila's cunt as it massaged my cock, made me go flat-out crazy. Sweat flew off my forehead and onto Lila's creamy breasts as I jacked into her like a man possessed. She came wildly in short order, squeezing her thighs against my hips and digging her fingers into my butt muscles as she surged against me. Recalling how much the girls had loved the taste of my cream the day before, I pulled out of Lila at the last moment and shot my seed all over her heaving body. Jeri withdrew her thumb from my ass so she could rub my sticky cream into Lila's skin as the two women kissed.

Before sunset, I escorted the girls back to their room at the lodge, where we exchanged phone numbers and goodbyes. They checked out the following morning with a standing offer from me: free ski lessons, anytime.

Three's Company

Natalie Clark

As I sat at the vanity in my bedroom, looking in the mirror and applying makeup, I heard the door of my apartment open and close. I smiled at my reflection, checking the pink gloss on my lips and running my fingers through my auburn hair. My boyfriend, Jared, was home and a thrill of arousal coursed through me. It still did every time I thought about him, even though we'd been together almost a year.

I walked out of the bedroom and let out a surprised gasp when I saw who was actually in the kitchen.

Jared's friend Shawn was poking through our fridge. He turned to face me with a bottle of beer in one hand. "Oh, hi. I didn't think you were home."

"Uh, yeah. I live here." I didn't mind Shawn having a key to our apartment. He watered the plants and fed our cat when we went away. But I did mind that he seemed to be there more and more frequently without invitation, even as I began noticing his hot body.

"Whatever. Help yourself." I went into the living room, sitting down on the couch with a magazine while I awaited Jared's return. I wanted to go on the date we'd planned, but even more than that, I was frantic to fuck my boyfriend for the first time in days. Our schedules had been crazy that week, allowing us only enough time to exchange hellos and goodbyes as we passed through the apartment. I hoped Shawn would have sense enough to leave after Jared got home.

Shawn came out of the kitchen with a sandwich and beer, and flopped down on a chair. He took charge of the remote, turning the TV to ESPN.

I flipped through my magazine, but continually snuck surreptitious glances at Shawn. His denim-clad legs were spread wide. I couldn't help checking out his package and wondering how his cock compared to Jared's. Little did I know that I'd soon find out.

Fifteen awkward minutes passed, during which a heightened sense of awareness grew between us. I'd always thought Shawn was attractive, and from the glances I intercepted, I gathered he thought the same about me. After a few minutes, I looked up from my magazine to catch him staring at my legs. And when I glanced over a second time, his eyes were trained on my cleavage. It would've been skeevy if I wasn't doing the exact same thing, gawking at his body on the sly.

When the apartment door opened, announcing Jared's arrival, I jumped and my heart sped up, as if I'd been caught doing something wrong. I rose from the couch to welcome him home, throwing my arms around him and giving him a big kiss and hug. "Shawn's here," I announced as if Jared couldn't see that.

The two guys muttered, "Hey, man," then Jared went to the kitchen for a beer. He passed one to me when he returned to the living room. We sat close together on the couch, sipping brews and watching TV.

My pussy was hungry and wanted attention. I'd waited all week for some together time with Jared, and I was going to have it if I had to drive Shawn out of the apartment with a broom. I figured the best way to give him the hint was to put on a PDA that left no doubt about my intentions for the rest of the evening.

I slid even closer to Jared, hooking one of my bare legs over his and cuddling up to his side. I kissed his neck, and ran my hand up and down his chest and stomach. First I teased him through his shirt, then I reached underneath, stroking his naked skin.

Unfazed by his friend's presence, Jared leaned in to kiss me. His mouth was wet and hot, and his tongue stroked mine seductively.

My hand slipped into his hair, pulling him even closer. I forgot about Shawn and concentrated on Jared's deep, scorching kiss. When we broke apart, I was breathless. Only then did I remember Shawn and looked over to catch his reaction.

His eyes shot back to the TV as he tried to pretend he hadn't been watching us. His feigned indifference spurred me to greater efforts. I climbed on Jared's lap, and we made out in a blatant display of horniness. I realized Jared wasn't really oblivious to Shawn's presence any more than I was. On some level, we were putting on a show for his benefit.

After more passionate kissing and heated groping of my ass,

Jared pulled away from sucking on my throat. "Baby, we do have a guest. What do you think of Shawn joining us?"

For a moment, I couldn't believe I'd heard him right. Could my secret fantasy of having two men at once possibly come true so easily? But Jared showed no sign that he was joking. We turned toward Shawn simultaneously.

He swallowed. "Seriously?"

"Haven't you ever wondered?" I asked. "I'll admit I have."

"Friends share," Jared added. "Besides, I think it's kinda hot."

Shawn set his empty bottle aside and walked over to the couch. He nervously perched on the arm closest to us. I turned toward him and leaned in, pressing my lips against his.

Aware of Jared watching, our first kiss was tentative. But when Jared showed no sign of jealousy and rubbed my thigh encouragingly, I kissed Shawn harder and deeper, wrapping my hand around the back of his neck and exploring his mouth with my tongue. The moment of unease passed, and I began to enjoy making out with another man right in front of my boyfriend. It was extremely sexy.

Shawn lost his inhibition and began to really get into it. His right hand cupped my face and his left roamed down my back to grab my ass. At the same time, Jared's hands stroked my bare thighs beneath my skirt, sliding all the way to my crotch. He slipped his fingers beneath the elastic of my underwear and caressed the plump lips of my aching pussy.

I was wet with arousal and ready for his touch. His fingers plunged inside my dripping channel, and my cunt greedily clenched them. He stroked in and out for several moments, then moved his fingers up to circle my clit.

I moaned into Shawn's mouth while thrusting my cunt toward

Jared's hand. The forbidden excitement of having sex with two men at once turned my desire from hot to fiery. Every caress seemed magnified. Shawn's kisses on my throat and across the swell of each breast, and Jared's fingers skillfully playing with my pussy both urged me toward ecstasy.

Shawn pulled off my shirt and resumed kissing my cleavage. His mouth worried a nipple through the sheer fabric of my bra, sucking until it was soaked. My dark areola showed through the wet material. Then Jared pulled down one cup to reveal my full breast and turgid tip. His mouth felt like wet fire as it surrounded the nipple and sucked hard. His hand never stopped moving on my cunt, rubbing my clit and then finger-fucking my hole.

Shawn unclasped and removed my bra, then both men resumed licking and sucking my tits. I put a hand on the back of each head, one dark and one light, and held them to my breasts. The tugging sensation on each nipple was supremely erotic. I moaned loudly and arched my back, forcing my boobs deeper into their mouths.

Jared's constant fingering of my pussy and the exotic delight of sharing myself with two men soon had my hips jerking. An explosion roared through me from my core to every nerve ending as I came hard and fast. I gripped their hair in my clutching fingers and cried out as my orgasm ripped through me. Finishing with a shudder, I slumped against Jared with my eyes closed. He rubbed my back and Shawn stroked my thigh.

After a moment, I recovered from the aftershocks and sat up, ready to give the two men their turn. I didn't need to look at the bulges in their jeans to know they were both hard and ready. The heat in each pair of eyes was enough to blister paint.

I slid off Jared's lap to take off my skirt and underpants, then stood for a moment, relishing the two gazes riveted on my nude body. Dropping to my knees, I reached for the zipper on Jared's fly and quickly released his straining cock. It burst forth from his pants into my waiting hand. I encircled it and rubbed the thick length up and down while Shawn watched. Leaning forward, I licked the entire shaft from balls to head. I looked up to see both men watching eagerly, their lips parted with passion.

I put on a real show, licking and sucking Jared's swollen prick while stroking it steadily with my hand. He let out a low groan, and Shawn's hand went to his groin, caressing his erection through his jeans.

After a few minutes, I let go of Jared's dick and unfastened Shawn's jeans. Pulling down his boxers, I freed his erection. My question from earlier was answered. His cock was longer and thinner than Jared's, and curved slightly to the left. I wondered how his shaft would feel inside me, and knowing that I'd probably find out soon was thrilling.

Again, I filled my mouth with a solid length of dick and sucked so hard my cheeks hollowed with the effort. As I gave attention to Shawn's cock with my mouth and hand, I reached out to stroke Jared again. It felt decadent and naughty to kneel on the floor pleasuring them both, and I loved it.

I spent some time moving between them, sucking one cock and then the other, but finally I made the men stand up and move close together so I could treat them simultaneously. I joined their dicks together, rubbing them against each other and stroking them with both my hands. Leaning in, I licked up and down their rigid shafts, teasing them one after the other. The pulsing flesh and taste of precome on my tongue drove me wild.

Above me, the guys groaned and their breathing rasped loudly. The pressure of one pair of hands was on my head, the other on my neck and shoulders. I licked and sucked until Jared and Shawn were shivering and ready to come.

I stopped and stood up, placing myself between them to enjoy a dual embrace. Wrapping my arms around Shawn's neck, I pulled him down to kiss me. My ass pushed back into Jared's erection, and I rubbed against it.

The heat of male bodies surrounded me. Their hands moved all over my naked skin, and their hard cocks temptingly brushed against me. I turned in the circle of arms to face Jared and kiss him, showing my appreciation for this delightful development in our sex life.

Shawn moved in behind me, his cock rubbing the groove of my asscheeks, and his mouth kissing and licking my shoulder. His hands stroked my hips and thighs, inflaming my lust.

The sensation of being held by two men at once was fantastic. It was making me dizzy with desire. The rough denim of Jared's jeans scraped my mound, and I pushed his pants farther down his hips. My breasts were squashed against Jared's hard chest, and both men held me tight.

Jared plunged his hands into my hair, holding my head steady while he kissed me hard and deep, then he pulled away to suggest we move to the bedroom.

We followed Jared's suggestion. In the bedroom, the men stripped, and I got an eyeful of two beautiful male bodies. Shawn and I lay down on the bed, but Jared sat at the foot. "Go ahead. I want to watch you fuck."

Shawn hesitated less than a second before moving in to kiss

me. His mouth was hot and wet, and his tongue swirled expertly inside my mouth, drawing out my response.

I ran my hand up his muscular chest, over his shoulder and to his neck, pulling him closer still. As we kissed, I was aware of Jared watching, even with my eyes closed. It boosted my excitement to know we were going to fuck right in front of my boyfriend.

After a few moments of feverish kissing and dry humping, Shawn pulled back. "I can't wait anymore," he panted.

We both glanced at Jared as if for permission to continue, and he nodded slightly.

Shawn reached down between us and guided his cock to my cunt. As he slipped inside, my eager pussy clenched around him, and I sighed with satisfaction.

Shawn's cock wasn't as thick as Jared's—nobody I'd ever dated had been as wide—but with that quirky twist to the left, I could really feel it inside me. When he plunged deeper, the head hit my G-spot like a heat-seeking missile striking its target. I moaned and arched against him.

Withdrawing and plunging in again, Shawn hit the exact same spot. This time I cried out loudly. The pleasure was too intense to hold it in. My eyes opened to gaze at Jared over Shawn's shoulder. His eyes were half closed in pleasure, and he was slowly stroking his cock.

Shawn's eyes were shut, and his brow furrowed in concentration as he pushed into me again and again, building up a delicious friction. Our earlier foreplay made it impossible for either of us to hold back for long.

Suddenly, Jared's voice cut across our groans and moans. "Wait! Not yet. I changed my mind. I want in on this." Jared reached for the tube of lubricant in the bedside table and slathered his cock with it. My heart raced with excitement. My anus clenched and released in anticipation of Jared fucking it.

Shawn rolled to his side, pulling me with him while keeping his dick inside my cunt, and Jared moved in behind me. My heart pounded with excitement as I prepared to be filled with two cocks at once.

With Jared's girth, it was always a tight fit when we had anal sex, leaving me a little sore afterward, but in a good way. He teased my anus open with the lubed tip of his finger and pumped it in and out of my ass. He added two, then three fingers, stretching me a little more.

I relaxed my muscles and grew accustomed to his thrusting digits. A moment later, Jared's fingers were replaced by the tip of his cock pushing inexorably inside. I held my breath as he pushed hard to slip his cock into my tiny, puckered hole. The ring of muscle gradually stretched, and once he slipped inside, I felt wonderfully filled. Shawn's cock still pulsed inside my pussy, and he thrust a little despite his attempts to hold back.

The feeling of being stuffed back and front by two big cocks was even better than I'd imagined it would be. My eyes closed as I savored the tension in my ass and pussy. Then the two men began to move, and the sensations suddenly intensified. Shawn pulled out and thrust back into my waiting channel. As his friend entered, Jared withdrew his thick length of dick before plunging back inside my asshole.

I lay between two walls of naked male flesh, burning with their heat and my desire. Jared's hand reached around my body to clutch and knead my breast. Shawn's face was buried in my shoulder. I was completely cocooned by their strong, handsome bodies.

Shawn moved faster, stroking in and out of my slippery cunt on a slick of fluids. Jared continued to work it, reaming my ass at a rapidly increasing pace. Each thrust was an effort, and he grunted as he forced his meat back into my tight channel. Shawn groaned continuously and breathed sharply when he bumped dicks with Jared through the thin wall of flesh deep inside me.

I sighed and moaned as the two men impaled me again and again with their tireless erections. It was so exhilarating, I couldn't hold back. In another moment, my orgasm rose inside me and burst. I screamed as I rode the wave of ecstasy, coming with a shaking intensity and filled to the limit with cock.

At almost the same moment, Shawn released his hot load. He shouted, bit down on my shoulder and shuddered fiercely against me. His cock pulsed with strong tremors inside my spasming pussy.

The onslaught of our mutual orgasm was too much for Jared. He broke loose, too, ramming into my ass hard and fast, and grunting like a caveman. He squeezed my tit as he thrust one last time, then he came, buried deep inside my body.

The three of us lay panting and sweating as we recovered from our ménage. I'd never felt such elation and knew I wanted to do this again.

After a bit, Jared pulled out and rolled onto his back. "What do you think?" he said, still sounding breathless.

"Unbelievable," Shawn said. "I never felt anything like that in my life."

I nodded in agreement. "I think we need to do it again to make sure it wasn't a fluke."

Jared rolled back toward me and kissed my shoulder. "You're insatiable," he murmured.

Later that evening after showers, drinks and pizza, I showed him just how insatiable I could be when I took on both men again.

This time we fucked on the living room floor. On my hands and knees, I faced Jared, who was sitting on the couch. I sucked his cock deep into my throat until my nose hit his pubic hair. Behind me, Shawn knelt with his cock buried to the hilt in my pussy. He thrust into me hard, driving my knees across the carpet and my face deeper into Jared's crotch. With my boyfriend's thick, hard shaft in my mouth and his friend's long, solid cock in my pussy, I couldn't have been happier. I was so aroused that I came, too, not long after the two men released their loads.

After that evening, Shawn continued to be a regular visitor at our apartment, but it no longer irritated me when he showed up unannounced. In fact, I learned to love it when an evening for two evolved into an evening for three.

Threesomes weren't always the main course of our sexual diet, but they added spice and a forbidden thrill several times a month. And when Shawn lost his key to the apartment, I gladly made him another copy.

Neighborhood Watch

JAKE SCHULTE

Some people believe in fate or destiny. I simply believe that everything happens for a reason. It was inevitable that Karen and Lynette would make love to each other, and it was my fortunate pleasure to be there last Friday when it happened.

Karen and I have been married for more than ten years. She is a short, voluptuous brunette with shoulder-length wavy hair and breasts that should be in the Louvre. Her lips are full and tender, and some of the best moments of my life have been those spent tasting that pout as her pink tongue explored my mouth. Curvy hips frame her nicely rounded ass, and her pussy is tight and juicy.

Lynette moved in next door about three months ago, and we all became best friends. She's in her early thirties, divorced and doesn't have any kids. Lynette is tall and thin, standing about a foot taller than Karen. She has long, shapely legs and a small, tight ass, the cheeks of which would fit perfectly in the palms of your hands. Her breasts are smaller than my wife's but look prominent on her petite frame. She wears her wheat-colored hair pulled back in a ponytail, and when it's not, she likes to brush it back with her fingers while she talks.

The two girls were sitting on the couch in our living room, and I was sitting across from them in a wingback chair with my feet up on the ottoman. I was looking up Lynette's short skirt, getting an eyeful of her purple panties and long, sleek thighs. Karen was wearing a pair of tight white shorts, and through the thin fabric, I could see the outline of her pussy and the dark shadow of her curly bush.

We were having a good time, being on our third, or maybe it was the fourth, round of vodka martinis. My head was spinning slightly, and I felt warm and relaxed. I visualized both of the girls naked, on top of each other, and my cock began to ache and swell in earnest at the thought.

Although different physically, both women have similar personalities. Each of them is a successful, independent businesswoman with an aggressive, outgoing personality. Sitting near each other on the couch, they were giggling and glancing over at me, and soon took note of my thickening cock, which was tenting my shorts.

"Are you having a good time looking up Lynette's skirt, honey?" Karen giggled.

"I was only trying to see what color panties she's wearing," I admitted, blushing.

"So, what color are my panties, Jake?" Lynette asked.

"Bright purple," I blurted out.

They broke into raucous laughter, their breasts jiggling enticingly as they giggled. They shared a look of recognition and amusement before turning back to me.

"I know him too well," Karen said.

"It's okay with you if he looks?" Lynette asked.

"Of course, I like to look, too," Karen said in a husky voice. She leaned over and gave Lynette a kiss on the cheek, and that's when it happened.

Lynette put down her drink and moved closer to my wife. She delicately placed her hands on Karen's cheeks. Sliding her fingers downward, tracing her smooth skin, she held my wife's face inches from hers. Ever so slowly, Lynette moved her ripe lips closer and closer. Karen's expression was full of surprise, and her breath came in short, ragged gasps. Lynette turned her head slightly and then pressed her lips against my wife's quivering mouth. It was the most gentle thing I had ever seen, like two beautiful flowers meeting.

Karen's throat moved slightly, and a soft whimper was absorbed by Lynette's inquiring mouth as their delicate kiss bonded them together, all for me to see.

My swollen cock was raging inside my shorts. Watching my wife and Lynette kiss sent an electric shock through my body that jerked my cock to its maximum length. Lynette removed her lips but still held Karen's face close to hers. Karen's eyes were wide and darted toward me with a look of concern.

"Is it all right if I kiss you again, Karen?" Lynette asked.

"I want you to," Karen said, glancing at me for my reaction.

I could see Karen's rock-hard nipples through her clothes,

and I merely nodded my head yes. I wanted to see these two luscious women make love.

Lynette kissed her again, and I saw Karen's mouth open wide to accept her girlfriend's tongue. My wife stroked Lynette's hair as she rose to her knees, so that their bodies were now pressing against each other, with their lips locked together and their tongues exploring each other's mouths. My wife's larger breasts pressed against Lynette's smaller ones as they embraced tightly, drawn into sexual abandon by their passionate kisses. Lynette finished their lip-lock and began to lightly kiss my wife on the cheek before moving down to her neck. She sucked and kissed my wife's exposed flesh, while her fingers boldly moved to the top button on Karen's blouse.

Lynette unfastened each button deliberately, until Karen's blouse parted to expose her white bra and toned stomach. She deftly slipped the blouse off Karen's shoulders, and my wife's full figure came into view. Her lacy bra was stretched to maximum capacity by her magnificent breasts.

Lynette pulled her own blouse over her head and tossed it on the floor. She was wearing a purple bra to match her panties, and her sizeable nipples were clearly erect beneath her delicate undergarment, outlining her increasing desire.

"Let's strip together," Lynette said, reaching around to unclasp her bra. Karen hesitated, and then Lynette said, "Come on, baby. I want to touch those big tits." Lynette unhooked her bra but held it together, waiting for my wife to join her.

Karen looked at me, wordlessly questioning if she should take this final step. I stood up and pulled my shirt over my head. Quickly, I pulled down my shorts and jockeys. My long, thick cock sprang upward. I sat back down in the chair, with my heavy balls on display and my throbbing cock waving in the air. Karen smiled, my actions giving her the answer she needed. My wife reached around and unhooked the back of her bra, still holding the ends behind her back like Lynette.

"Now, let's do it together," Lynette said lustily, slowly sliding a delicate shoulder strap down and revealing the top of her left breast.

Karen pulled her bra down until only her thick brown nipples were covered, and then both women dropped their bras to the floor. I was mesmerized by the difference and quality of their breasts. Lynette's medium-sized breasts were white and firm, with long, pointed pink nipples jutting out from small areolas. In contrast, Karen's large, olive-toned breasts had giant areolas, with short, thick brown nipples. They kissed again, this time letting their tongues linger as they sensually explored each other with their naked breasts pressed together.

Lynette began slowly stroking the tops of Karen's breasts. Moving her hands around, Lynette softly squeezed the fleshy orbs, rubbing her thumbs over my wife's stiff nipples. Karen moaned and placed her hands on Lynette's breasts, kneading them energetically. She softly tweaked the big pink nubs, and Lynette gasped with pleasure.

I couldn't take it any longer. I was overwhelmed with the sensuous scene before me. I began to stroke the length of my turgid prick, pulling the foreskin up and down over the plump head.

"Your husband's got a nice big cock," Lynette said as she unfastened Karen's shorts.

Karen smiled and watched me stroke my prick, while Lynette slid the shorts down over my wife's curvy hips. Karen was wearing a white thong that accentuated her plump asscheeks. Her brown bush was visible through the front of the sheer panties. Lynette stood up and pushed Karen back onto the couch. She reclined in front of us with a pillow under her head. Lynette unzipped her skirt and stepped out of it, revealing the purple bikini panties I had been so interested in earlier. She was long and sleek like a runner, I thought as I ogled her toned body.

Lynette looked at me stroking my cock and said, "Since you're letting me make love to Karen, I'll give you a show while I make her come."

She slid her fingers under the thin purple panties and pulled them down over her ass, past her hips and over her pubic mound. Her shaved pussy was pink, with an already hard clitoris poised at the top of her slit. I stroked my cock faster as she bent over my wife with her toned ass facing me.

Lynette lowered her face to my wife's lovely breasts, and her wet tongue circled one thick brown nipple. Karen sighed and rocked her head back against the pillow, lifting her breasts toward Lynette's hungry lips. Lynette took the wet nipple into her mouth and greedily sucked on it. Holding Karen's breast with both hands, she squeezed and sucked at the same time. Karen thrashed her head from side to side, moaning uncontrollably while Lynette devoured her nipple.

She leaned over my wife farther, then took the other nipple into her mouth and sucked on them both in turn as she held Karen's mounds in her hands. Lynette's pussy lips opened slightly as she bent over to worship my wife's heaving breasts, showing me the warm, wet flesh within.

"Oh fuck," I moaned, as I squeezed my cock more firmly. I stroked myself as slowly as my self-control allowed, not wanting to come early and miss any of the women's lovemaking.

Lynette lifted her head and smiled at me, confident that I was enjoying her spectacle. "If you think that's good, watch this."

She slid her hand down Karen's stomach toward her white panties. Karen's legs spread wider as Lynette's hand traveled along the smooth skin, nearing the waistband of the panties. Lynette's bright-red fingernails advanced along the see-through panel of the undies that was stretched tight over my wife's curly bush.

Karen was whimpering, and her legs quivered in anticipation of Lynette's delicate touch. Lynette's hands moved lightly around Karen's panty-clad pussy, stroking her inner thighs. Karen voiced a short groan of relief as Lynette cupped her mound with one hand, squeezing and stroking her hot pussy through the wet fabric.

Tracing Karen's opening with her finger, Lynette leaned forward and planted gentle kisses on the soaked panties covering the beautiful treasure she was seeking.

"Take them off. Lick her pussy," I exclaimed, urging Lynette to give us both what we wanted.

I stroked my cock faster as I watched Lynette peel off my wife's panties and marvel at the wet, succulent pussy before her.

"I'm going to make you feel so good, baby," Lynette said, as she lowered her lips to the sexy slit in front of her.

"I want to watch you. I want to see your tongue going inside me," Karen gasped.

Lynette began by hugging Karen's hips and planting soft kisses up and down the length of my wife's pussy. It must have felt like a butterfly traveling up and down her aroused flesh. Then her tongue darted out and penetrated the opening, plunging in and out like a small cock. My wife screamed again, and then lifted herself up, her large breasts swaying as she watched Lynette's tongue invade her hot pussy. While Lynette licked, she deftly inserted one digit and then two inside Karen.

She finger-fucked Karen slowly, and then faster and faster when her tongue found Karen's clit. Her fingers were slick and her face shiny, both covered with my wife's juices. Moving her head from side to side, Lynette licked and sucked on Karen's button, applying pressure with her lips while her fingers plunged in and out of my wife's hole. Lynette's buttocks flexed and released, and her pussy tightened and relaxed as she fucked Karen. I savored the sight of them experiencing such a sensual moment, and I stroked my cock even faster, feeling a familiar pleasure growing in my balls.

Karen was groaning and moaning in a continuous expression of pleasure as Lynette brought her to the most intense orgasm she had ever experienced. She released one long penetrating scream, and her pussy tightened around Lynette's fingers as her body went rigid.

I stroked my cock with increasing speed. My wife turned to look at me, and her chestnut hair fell across her beautiful face. I watched as a jet of semen exploded out of my shaft, splattering my chest. I stroked myself harder and encouraged a second and third eruption of cream, as I grunted and emptied my balls onto myself until it looked like I was covered with suntan lotion.

Afterward, I headed to the bathroom to wash up, and as I toweled off, I heard laughter coming from the bedroom. The women were in our king-size bed, and when I walked in, I was treated to the sight of my wife's shapely ass poised up in the air as she lowered her head between Lynette's legs. Lynette was lying on her back, and her legs were spread wide to allow Karen full access to her shaved cunt. Her pink pussy was wet with excitement. Karen moved closer and planted a soft kiss on Lynette's mound. As she leaned forward, my wife's sweet pussy came into view.

Karen covered Lynette's sex with tantalizing kisses. It looked like she was an expert pussy-eater, even though it was the first time for her. She moaned in ecstasy as her tongue slipped into Lynette's wet entrance. Lynette moved her arms over her head and stretched, savoring the feeling of my wife's tongue dancing on her pussy.

I quickly developed another raging hard-on watching my wife be the aggressor as she licked and sucked her new lover. I saw her own moisture trickling from her cunt, and I immediately knew that she was aroused more than she had been in years.

"Put your cock in her, Jake, and fuck her while she kisses me down there," Lynette ordered, as if she were directing an adult film.

Karen pushed her ass up in invitation, and I was more than willing to comply. I got on my knees behind her and rubbed the bulbous head of my cock up and down her dripping slit, covering it with her juices before smoothly sliding inside her.

"Don't come in her. I'm not through with her yet," Lynette moaned, as Karen found her sweet spot.

Karen had slipped two of her fingers into Lynette's cunt and was now finger-fucking her rhythmically as she licked and sucked on Lynette's clit. My wife was lost in sexual abandon, with her face deep in Lynette's pussy and my cock buried to the hilt in her slit. She pushed back against me, and I thrust in and out of her. She rapidly licked Lynette's clit, applying pressure with her lips and tongue. Lynette began to pant, pushing her pussy up into my wife's face as she quickly raced toward fulfillment.

"Take your cock out and put it in my mouth," Lynette groaned. "I want to taste Karen's pussy when I come."

I pulled out and moved around until my cock was near Lynette's face. Karen looked up, and I could tell she was watching me while she sucked her friend's clit. My wife's face was slick with Lynette's juices, and the scent of pussy had perfumed the room.

"Give it to me now. In my mouth," Lynette begged, and she opened her lips eagerly to receive my cock.

She turned her head toward me, and I slipped the first three inches of my dick into her mouth. Lynette greedily sucked my cock as Karen increased the pressure and speed of her lips and tongue on Lynette's clit. Lynette was moaning around my shaft, and she sucked on me hard, sliding her lips rapidly up and down the length of my cock.

Pulling away for a moment, Lynette said to Karen, "I can taste you on his dick, baby, and it's so good."

Then she gobbled me up again, and I began to squeeze and fondle her breasts, rolling the stiff pink nipples between my fingers. She sucked more of my staff into her mouth to show her appreciation. My wife slurped noisily at Lynette's pussy, and her fingers made squishing noises as they plunged in and out of her lover. Lynette's nipples were rock-hard between my fingers, and I tugged on them, pinching her nubs softly. Her legs began to quiver, and her mouth tightened on my cock as she moaned loudly around it. Karen finished her off with several short sucks on her engorged clit. Lynette's muffled shrieks ebbed and flowed along with her orgasm until she went limp.

Karen continued to softly kiss Lynette's pussy, while she slowly came back down to earth. Lynette continued to suck my cock, even through her intense orgasm, causing me to climax. Meanwhile Karen, unwilling to give up the sweet taste of pussy, continued to plant tender kisses on Lynette's slick sex.

After Karen and Lynette made love to each other that afternoon, our lives changed forever. Over the last few months, the three of us have explored every sexual position there is. I know that it can't last forever and that Lynette will eventually go her own way, but right now, Karen and I are happier than ever.

Tempting Trios

Tracy Saunders

The bar was half empty, which was unusual for a Friday night. Maybe it was the weather reports; they'd been threatening thunderstorms for two days now, and the sky was dark and heavy with clouds. Still, this was the longest I'd ever sat nursing a glass of wine without being approached by some random guy on the prowl. I realized that I could have gone straight home after work, but the thought of a microwaved dinner in front of the TV wasn't very enticing. So there I was, with a nearly empty glass in front of me, looking for company, or at least someone to buy my next drink.

It usually isn't too difficult to make happen because men are generally attracted to my long auburn hair, green eyes and trim body. And having large breasts doesn't hurt. That night, I was wearing a tight

V-neck sweater that accentuated my most arresting feature, but still, no fish would bite, so I finally broke down and ordered myself another glass of Riesling.

That's when my luck changed. As I was pulling my wallet from my purse, a man sidled up to me and said, "I'll get that." I turned to thank him for the drink and was pleased with what I saw. Tall, dark and handsome in a navy business suit, he had wavy hair, a chiseled jaw and blue eyes that sparkled as he spoke. "I'm Jim," he said. "And you are?"

I introduced myself and shook his hand, my nipples growing hard in response to his firm, masculine grip. Already I could imagine that hand on my breast, or my thigh, or my cunt. He took the seat next to mine and we chatted a bit—basic getting-to-know-each-other stuff. When our glasses were drained I figured he'd make his move, either suggesting we go back to his place or mine. I wasn't expecting a third option.

"I have this friend," he started, and my heart sank as I waited for him to tell me about the down-on-his-luck coworker he was trying to set up. I looked around, expecting to find a guy waving at me from a table across the room, but the bar was still pretty desolate and no one made such a gesture. "No, he's not here," Jim said, seeing my bewilderment. "It's just that we have this arrangement. When one of us meets someone we like, we share. And I like you. Are you interested?"

Two guys? A threesome? Though I'd never considered it before, it sounded pretty good to me. My body was telling me to go for it; my pussy was starting to moisten. Jim paid my tab as I nodded my assent, and without another word I rose and followed him outside. He got into his car and I got into mine, and I couldn't believe what I was doing as

I tried not to lose sight of the silver sedan that was leading me to a new adventure.

Eventually, we pulled up to a condominium complex, where I parked in a space right beside Jim's car and turned off the ignition, while he got out and walked over. Taking my hand, he helped me out of my car, then led me to the door of one of the units and rang the bell. However, instead of waiting for someone to answer it, he turned the knob and walked right in. It was evident that he didn't live there, and just wanted to let the owner—who was obviously expecting us—know that we had arrived.

My heart skipped a beat when I saw Robert. He was also tall and handsome, but a little slimmer, with blond hair and green eyes. The knowledge that these two hunks were about to ravage me sexually reignited the fire in my cunt, and I was suddenly very glad that I'd accepted Jim's invitation. Having seen my other partner, I was now ready to hop right into bed, but first, our host showed us to the living room where a bottle of wine was already open and breathing. There, over glasses of Rioja, the men took some time to get to know me and told me a bit about themselves, which put me totally at ease.

In fact, I was so relaxed that I was the one who suggested we take the next step. Neither man disagreed, so I followed Robert upstairs, with Jim bringing up the rear. Since I was still standing between them when we entered the bedroom, Robert turned around, touched my jaw and tilted my face to his. As we kissed, my tongue slip-sliding against his, Jim cupped my breasts from behind and rubbed his thumbs over my nipples, which throbbed at his touch. He abandoned my tits to unbutton my blouse, and I was soon standing there in nothing but my skirt and a lacy black bra.

Jim unzipped my skirt while Robert worked at the front clasp of my bra, and then I was naked, though both men remained clothed. They spent a moment admiring my nude form, and I knew they were pleased with what they saw from both the front view and the rear. Robert couldn't tear his eyes from the trimmed triangle of hair covering my mound, while his friend reverently stroked my asscheeks. I felt like a goddess being worshipped, and although I enjoyed being the sole object of all this male attention, I wanted to see what the men looked like out of their clothes.

Beginning with the one standing in front of me, I pulled his sweater over his blond head. I could hear rustling from behind and figured that Jim was taking off his shirt, having shed his suit jacket in the living room. I admired Robert's faintly muscled chest before glancing back to check out Jim. He was brawnier and nude, with an impressive cock that stuck out straight from beneath a patch of dark, wiry curls. Similar curls ringed his erect nipples; I turned around to flick the tiny nubs with my tongue while Robert removed the rest of his clothes.

I heard the sound of a belt buckle hitting the floor and then scraping along it as jeans were kicked off and swept aside, and then I felt a hard dick pressing up against my ass. Insistently, it worked its way between my rear cheeks before coming to rest. Robert nuzzled the nape of my neck, his shaft pulsing against my flesh as I took Jim's cock in my hand. As I pumped it up and down, a moan escaped his lips, which were pressed firmly against mine. While we kissed wildly, Robert reached around me, ran a finger between my labia, and then rubbed circles over my hard little button.

Soon, both men were groaning loudly, and I was making quite

a few noises of my own. The pressure of Robert's fingers grew more insistent, until my hips began to writhe. I needed to feel this man inside me; no, I needed to feel them both, so I slipped away from the hands massaging my pussy and got down on my knees. I was still holding Jim's dick, and I opened my mouth wide to wrap my lips around his knob. As I swabbed the flesh with my tongue, Robert lowered himself behind me and then moved my body into position to receive him doggie-style.

Jim sat down on the edge of the bed, and I placed one hand flat on the floor, keeping the other wrapped around the base of his erection. I bobbed my head back and forth so that my tongue slid along his length, and I drew my lips in tightly to create a firm lock around his shaft. His fingers tangled in my hair as I swallowed him again and again, and then my pussy mimicked my throat by opening up to take in the whole length of Robert's dick. His balls brushed my asscheeks when he reached my core and remained pressed up against me as he rested there momentarily. He might have been taking a breather, but I sure as hell wasn't; I continued sucking down Jim's cock without missing a beat.

I kept up my ministrations as Robert began sawing in and out of my cunt, and I even managed to time my movements on Jim's dick with his. We all moved together in sync; as I swallowed one cock down my throat, another one pressed forward and filled my pussy. Then, when I drew my head back along Jim's length until only the tip remained lodged between my lips, Robert pulled his cock from between my legs, leaving me almost empty inside. Their actions were repeated again and again, until the men decided that it was time for a change.

Jim slowly withdrew his dick from my mouth, a long string of saliva briefly prolonging our connection before it broke. After letting go of him, I placed both hands on the floor to steady myself, because Robert was now fucking me even harder. He punctuated his rapid thrusts with sharp smacks on my ass, obviously putting on a show. I didn't protest because the spanking actually turned me on even more. His hips rocked back and forth as he speared my moist cunt from behind, and though I expected Jim to do something, too, he just continued to watch while slowly stroking his dick.

I lunged forward in an attempt to recommence the blow job, but he moved out of the way, explaining that my mouth felt too good and he wasn't ready to come yet. Though I missed sucking him off, I let him have his way and concentrated on his friend. Robert dug his fingers into my hips as he plunged his cock into my tight canal, and soon he was fucking me so hard that my breasts bobbled wildly on my chest. My juices, which had never stopped flowing, ran down my thighs, and I grew hotter by the second. Then finally something inside me exploded. I announced my orgasm with a wild cry and pressed my legs together, hoping that would make Robert come, too.

Granting my wish, he grunted loudly and filled me with his cream. I could feel it coating my insides, and when he abruptly pulled out, his semen mingled with my fluids to drip down my inner thighs. Robert moved away quickly, which surprised me, but I understood why when Jim immediately took his place and thrust his dick into my sloppy cunt. When it was in my mouth, I hadn't realized that his tool was thicker and blunter than Robert's. My muscles had to stretch to receive this new meat. I was still in the throes of my orgasm, so my pussy shuddered around his shaft until it, too, pulsed and filled me with another load of warm semen.

Jim remained buried in my cunt until his balls were completely spent, while Robert stood to the side and watched. Having all reached our climaxes, we washed up and got dressed, and then Jim and I said goodbye to our host. It had been quite an interesting night, and I truly meant it when I told them both I would be happy to come again.

I thought about my experience with Jim and Robert over the following days, even masturbated to the memories of it. However, instead of seeing two cocks in these scenarios, I saw two pussies and two pairs of breasts. So I called Robert, because I'd felt a closer bond with him, and not only was he happy to hear from me, he said he knew a woman whom he was certain I would like.

A week later, I returned to Robert's condominium, this time on my own. Though I would have also liked to see Jim again, my pussy tingled at the thought of having sex with another woman as well as a man. And when I met Megan for the first time, I was glad I'd made that choice. She was petite, with a trim figure and short blonde hair, dressed casually in jeans and a tight sweater that hugged her small breasts. Once again, an uncorked bottle of wine was on the table, but I was too excited to take more than a few sips. Seeing that, Robert stood, took each of us by the hand and led us up to the bedroom.

He knew I'd never been with another woman before, so he took the lead by stripping off my clothes. I slipped out of my shoes as he pulled my top up over my head, and I was surprised to feel another pair of hands behind me working the hooks of my bra. Apparently Megan was more experienced at this sort of thing, because as soon as I was topless she cupped my breasts. But now, instead of rough male fingers rubbing my erect nipples, the touch was slow and gentle. Meanwhile, Robert helped me out of my jeans and underwear, and then we turned to undress Megan together.

As Robert stripped, I tentatively reached out and stroked Megan, delighting in the feel of her smooth skin beneath my fingertips. Taking my hand in hers, she pressed it firmly to her breast, encouraging me to give it a good, hard squeeze. Robert watched, remaining silent, as she wrapped her arms around my waist to pull me closer to her, and when our bodies met she pressed her lips to mine. The kiss was chaste at first, but when I felt her tongue at my lips I opened wide to let it inside. Our embrace quickly grew more passionate, our tits and pussies mashing together, my auburn curls interlaced with her blonde ones.

Megan was clutching my asscheeks, holding my body so tightly to hers that Robert had to pry us apart to join in the fun. He knelt between us as we continued kissing, and he turned his head from side to side as he took turns pressing his mouth to our cunts. Periodically, his tongue snaked between my lips to flick at my clit, and then I'd feel nothing for a moment as he did the same to her. Every time he tickled her button, she jerked in my arms, and I realized that I wanted to be the one giving her so much pleasure. I had never gone down on a woman before, so this was my big chance.

I joined Robert on the floor, and as we kissed, I could taste a mixture of her musk and mine on his lips. Even more anxious for a taste of Megan's cunt, I turned my head and moved my hand to her sex. I parted her labia with my thumb and index finger. Her clitoris had popped out from under its hood, and all I had to do was stretch out my tongue and press it against my target. When I did, her body quivered, so I reached my free hand around to hold on to her ass and then gave her another lick. This time, she let out a moan and grasped at the back of my head, mashing my mouth to her sex as Robert urged me on by murmuring dirty words in my ear. My appetite flourished, so I licked and sucked her even harder, swallowing the juices that flowed from her hole.

It wasn't long before Megan's body began to quake and I could hear her whimpering above me. She ground her pussy against my tongue as she shivered and shook, letting me know what it was like to make a woman come with my mouth. When she'd had enough, Robert pulled me away from her cunt and moved me into a crouching position on the bed. He knelt before me, offering me his erection. Opening wide, I swallowed his cock down, conscious that it had only been a week since the last time I'd done that very same thing, but to his friend while he looked on.

Now Megan watched as I sucked Robert's dick, though she didn't stay passive for long. Positioned on the mattress beside me, she licked his gently swaying balls while I dragged my lips back and forth along his length. Then she worked herself between us, through our legs, and stretched out on her back, lifting her head until her mouth was at my cunt. Slipping her tongue between my labia, she began eating me just like I'd eaten her. I groaned when she flicked at my clit, making my throat vibrate around Robert's shaft. In response, he jerked forward and drove his dick in even farther.

Then Robert pulled his prick from my mouth and moved between Megan's widely spread thighs. I watched as he grasped the base of his cock and positioned the head between her pussy lips. Raising her hips off the bed, she gave him better access to her hole, so he slowly eased himself inside. I watched her swollen labia engulf his shaft inch by inch, until he was completely buried in her cunt. That's when I caught Robert's gaze as he looked at me to see what I was going to do next.

I crawled closer to Robert and got up on my knees so that one was on either side of Megan, straddling her waist. I grabbed the back of his head, pulled his face to mine and kissed him hard. As my tongue slithered into his open mouth, I reached around him with my other hand and took hold of his asscheek. Then, with a firm grip, I helped guide him in and out of Megan's slippery cunt. Her hands moved to my hips, stroking my skin, then more roughly kneading my buttcheeks as she whispered how much she liked my heart-shaped ass. I could feel the muscles in his buttocks flex every time he pressed inside her, and my own pussy, long neglected, demanded the same attention. So the next time Robert pulled his length from Megan's cunt, I wrapped my fingers around the base of his cock and carefully repositioned him at my nether lips, then leaned back with my hands supporting my weight.

With a shove, he filled me with his dick and gave me a few good thrusts. Then he pulled back out and thrust into Megan a couple of times. He continued like that for a while, moving back and forth between our cunts as he fucked us both at the same time. The excitement of watching him go from me to another woman who was between my legs was truly exhilarating. My arousal kept on building, going higher and higher until Megan finally sent me over the edge.

It happened while Robert was pistoning his dick in and out of me. Reaching up, she spread my asscheeks and then nuzzled a fingertip against my asshole. I let out a cry as my insides burst and my cunt closed around Robert's shaft. It became difficult for him to move as I rode the waves of my orgasm, so he remained buried inside me until I'd relaxed somewhat. Then he pulled his prick from my pussy and plunged it right into Megan, fucking her until she was coming, too. Her small breasts bobbed as she writhed between our legs, giving him a good massage with her pussy, bringing him to the brink. He pulled out of her and let loose his cream. He managed to spray us both with ribbons of pearly white come as he finally reached his orgasm.

When he was finished, Megan and I thanked him by putting on a little show. We licked up the semen, covering each other's stomachs, breasts, pussies and thighs. He responded with a round of applause, and then retrieved the leftover wine from the living room while we lounged in bed. We toasted to our future fun, and whether my next adventure ends up being with Robert, Megan, Jim or partners I've yet to meet, I'm looking forward to being part of another sexy trio.

Switching Teams

Dana Grant

My husband, Sean, always goes crazy whenever he sees two attractive women kissing in a movie or walking hand in hand along the street. The magazines that he reads—the adult ones, that is—are full of girl-on-girl action. Sean gets horny in an instant if he sees feminine flesh touching feminine flesh, especially if it's nipple touching nipple.

I can see the beauty in two women kissing. I've always had an open mind about sexual matters, and I've even enjoyed having three-somes. It all started when Sean suggested that he'd like to watch me make out with another girl. About a year ago, he checked out a website frequented by swingers looking to hook up and arranged for us to meet a pretty blonde at a motel on the outskirts of the city where we live. I only insisted on one thing. Our marital bed was strictly for the two of us. If we wanted to fool around with strangers, then we had to do it away from home.

Our encounter with the blonde proved to be the first of several wonderful threesomes that we shared with various girls. We would always meet up at the same motel. I'd dance with the girl and strip her naked, then I would go down on her. Sean would get so hot watching me perform oral sex that it would quickly develop into a threesome. He'd penetrate her while I kissed her lips and breasts, then we'd wait until he was hard again, so that he could fuck me while our new friend did the kissing.

The reason why we love having threesomes is that our sex life is always better just before and afterward. We both fantasize plenty about what could happen when we meet with the girl, and we then take those fantasies into the bedroom with us. Afterward, things are even better, since each girl seems to teach us something new that we then incorporate into our love life. Take that blonde we met the first time around. By watching her licking my clit and pussy, Sean learned how to truly make me go wild. The oral sex that he's performed since then has proved that he's learned his lesson well.

In fact, Sean has discovered a lot about my erogenous zones, thanks to watching me with my female lovers. Sadly, I haven't learned quite so much about how his body works, so I suggested something different for our next encounter.

"Next time, why don't we do it with another guy?" I said to him while he was sitting in front of the television watching football. I think my suggestion surprised him a little, but I soon brought him around to my way of thinking. With my gentle encouragement, Sean soon acknowledged that the players onscreen had good bodies and that he admired them for their physical prowess. When I asked if he would like to touch and get closer to one of those bodies, he went silent for a moment, before admitting that maybe he would. I continued my argument by saying that just like he enjoyed watched two gorgeous girls together, I might also enjoy seeing two sexy men getting up close. He shyly agreed that it was only fair for us to try it out.

Later that night, I took out a small vibrator, lubed it up and then used it to penetrate Sean's behind. He groaned with joy as I pumped his cock while titillating his asshole with the vibe. When he got close to orgasm, I told him to imagine that it was a man who was fucking his ass, and he came hard, then collapsed in a sweaty, sticky heap on the bed.

The next morning, Sean went online. Before I knew it, he'd arranged for us to meet up with a bisexual guy named Jake. Jake was a bodybuilder, and it was easy for me to understand why Sean had chosen to respond to his ad. Jake's handsome face and sculpted muscles turned me on something fierce, and I couldn't wait to see him and my husband naked.

No sooner had Jake arrived at the motel than he started to strip off his clothing, getting ready for action. Sean stood slightly at a distance while half-clad Jake and I made small talk. He flattered us both by saying how nice it was for him to hook up with a couple where he found both the man and the woman equally attractive. I looked across at Sean and saw him blushing at the compliment. Sean didn't see me looking, though—he only had eyes for Jake's powerful body.

Then something happened that really surprised me. "Let's get this show on the road," Sean announced, and then he walked right up to Jake. Normally, it was left to me to get things started. It's always awkward meeting strangers and getting down to sex, but this time Sean had the whole thing under control. It was like he knew it was his turn to perform for me.

I sat on the bed and watched as my husband ran his hands across Jake's prominent pectorals. He touched them somewhat cautiously at first, as if he wasn't quite sure if he was doing it right. Jake helped to put him at ease by telling him how good his hands felt. For my part, I helped by lifting up my skirt and fingering my pussy. The all-man action was making me incredibly hot, and when Sean looked across and saw the effect that it was having on me, he became a lot more confident. Now, as well as fondling Jake's muscles, he was leaning in and sucking on his tiny nipples. Sean ran his fingers down Jake's back and then cupped his hands around his asscheeks. Jake was still in his underwear, but not for too much longer, because soon Sean was pushing them down his muscular thighs.

Sean dropped to his knees so that he was now staring right at Jake's substantial cock. I instantly felt the front of my panties getting wetter. It was big in its flaccid state and quickly grew bigger as Sean turned his attention to it. He planted kisses just below Jake's cock-head, then brushed his lips down along the shaft until he was licking the bodybuilder's balls. I looked on happily as Sean opened his mouth wider until the whole sac was between his lips.

A few sucks later, Jake's prick had fully stiffened. Pleased with that, I got off the bed, removed my panties and then joined my husband. It was amazing to think that I was kneeling alongside Sean while one of us sucked on Jake's hefty cock and the other licked his balls. It was definitely happening, though. I didn't have to pinch myself to make sure, because Sean beat me to it. Although he was concentrating hard on the balls in his mouth, he still found a way to grope my ass. He ran his left hand across my cheeks while his other hand stroked Jake's tree-trunk thighs. It was almost as if Sean was comparing the two of us—enjoying the softness of my tender flesh contrasted with Jake's rock-solid muscularity. I don't know which one of us came out on top, but I do know that together Jake and I had what it took to get my husband hard.

As I plunged my lips down Jake's erection, I also slid my hand inside my husband's pants. He wasn't wearing any underwear that night, so my fingers met with nothing but his swollen prick. Tightening them around Sean's shaft, I began to jerk him off in a determined manner. My fingers really tugged at his foreskin, making it chafe against his bulbous crown. I wanted him to get as hot as possible, because the throbbing of Jake's cock against my lips told me that he was ready to fuck my husband's ass.

I gave the bodybuilder's dick one final suck before my husband and I rose. I quickly opened Sean's fly and tugged down his pants. That allowed me to lean forward and wrap my lips around the head of Sean's cock. He was rock hard; it was time for Jake to take over.

I pulled my mouth off my husband before he could come and reached for some lube. Then I returned to Sean and knelt behind him. Jake wrapped his arms around my husband, and the two men kissed while I worked the lube into Sean's anus. I slipped my fingers inside, and Sean moaned into Jake's mouth as I thrust my slick digits in and out to prepare him for Jake. Then once his muscles seemed relaxed enough to accommodate Jake's erection, I told Jake that the time had come and the boys climbed onto the mattress.

It was the moment that I had been looking forward to the

most. When Jake penetrated my husband's behind, I was sure that it would open up a whole new world of sexual exploration for us. Just as Sean had learned many new tricks from watching me with women, I would learn some of my own from watching Jake screw Sean. In fact, as Jake moved up close to my husband's ass and slotted his prick between his cheeks, I was already dreaming of the day when I would fuck Sean with my very own strap-on.

Hurriedly, I repositioned myself underneath my husband. I wanted to see the look of pleasure on his face as his asshole received its first taste of cock. When the moment came, it was all that I had hoped it would be. Sean leaned toward me as he reveled in the ecstasy of penetration. We began to kiss: Sean with his eyes shut, while mine stayed open so I could see the contorted look of exhilaration on his face. His features had scrunched up tight into a ball as he savored the sensation of Jake's massive prick sliding deep inside his asshole.

Jake had plenty of power, and each time he pumped his hips back and forth, the force jostled our bodies. Sean was sandwiched between the fleshy cushion of my breasts and Jake's rock-hard pectorals, his asshole being continually penetrated by the bodybuilder's dick. I could feel Sean's cock pressed against my body. As soon as he was hard enough, I maneuvered him inside my pussy, and then I let the bodybuilder's thrusting motions cause Sean to plunge deep inside me.

Right then, Jake was the boss. His cock was repeatedly penetrating Sean's back passage, and the resulting effect made Sean's dick shoot in and out of my cunt. Although the physical pleasure that it caused me was immense, I tried to stay focused on the mental pleasure that the threesome was bringing. I thought of all those times Sean had sat watching football on television, or had stood in the shower after tennis staring at the physiques of the men around him. Maybe he'd always longed to have sex with another guy, and it was such a thrill to know that I had helped him live out that dream. And I'm sure it was even better for him to have me there with him. He could look straight into my eyes and feel my tits squashed against his chest at the same time that his ass was filled with cock. Another man's penis might have been working its way in and out of his back passage, but straight ahead was the woman he loved, a pair of red lips and a pussy that he could penetrate.

Spasms shot through my cunt and echoed in my clit as Sean's dick pushed in and out. Overwhelmed, I wrapped my arms around my husband and squeezed his ass, and then I reached a little further and caressed Jake's rock-solid thighs. Both guys' crotches were lurching in staccato thrusts, like they were being worked by a piston pump. In truth, though, it was Jake's extreme athleticism that was doing all the work. He just kept piling on the speed and power as he drove the three of us toward orgasm.

As the bodybuilder's thrusts grew ever stronger, a noisy groan squeezed right out of my throat. My pussy throbbed as it gave way to the overwhelming levels of stimulation that I was experiencing. Suddenly I was moaning, but despite that, I could still hear the slurping sounds made by my husband's cock forcing its way in and out of my quivering hole.

I kissed Sean hard on the lips because the power and circumstances of my orgasm made me love him more than ever. Feeling his dick filling my cunt, while watching him getting pleasured by Jake, had driven me to a level of fulfillment that was quite beyond anything I had ever known before. Then, at that very moment, Sean's cock began to pulse as his body responded in the only way it knew how. Each contraction of his balls forced a jet of come into my pussy, and his spasming refused to die away for a good long while.

Sean's lengthy orgasm owed plenty to Jake's dick, which continued to thrust in and out of my husband's anus. That was even better for me because as he built up to his own release, Jake worked his hands between Sean and me to tweak an erect nipple. His thick fingers squeezed the tip of my breast firmly enough to make me come again. My second orgasm coincided with the magical moment when Jake's prick began to spill its load inside my husband's asshole. His fingers tightened on my nipple as we reached our climaxes.

Jake's climax was silent, but I could tell that it was happening by the look of ecstasy that was etched upon Sean's features. He had closed his eyes and was muttering, "Yeah, oh yeah," to himself as he no doubt felt his asshole being overflowed with the bodybuilder's cream. He dug his fingers hard into my asscheeks, and when I kissed his neck, I noticed that his flesh was suddenly a mass of goose bumps.

Sean was experiencing the kind of orgasm that I had experienced during our first threesome. He'd discovered the joy of being pleasured not just by the person he loved, but also, and at the same time, by someone of the same sex—someone who had an intimate knowledge of the exact workings of the male body.

Still high from the intensity of his orgasm, Sean withdrew from my pussy and turned around to face Jake. When the bodybuilder kissed my husband on the mouth, a look of complete contentment spread across Sean's face.

Later that night, Sean confessed that the evening had gone way beyond what he'd been expecting. He couldn't get enough of the way that Jake had used his cock to stimulate his ass. "He really knew what buttons to press back there," he told me a hundred times over.

It was great for me to know that Sean had gotten so much out of our night with Jake and, consequently, that our future trips to the motel might be a little more varied than they had been in the past. For sure, my husband still loves to watch me make love to another woman. But having watched him playing around with a guy, I can more easily understand that obsession, and it's also good to know that the tables can be turned now and again, keeping us both satisfied.

Secret Fantasies

ALISON TYLER

I was late for work again. I could feel Marcus watching me, and when I looked over at him, he was smiling. "You're like a cartoon," he said with a grin. "Moving in fast-motion." He likes to watch me get ready for my day, even when I'm not in a rush. But when he tried to corner me in the bedroom that morning and kiss the back of my neck, I shrugged him away.

"I'm late," I insisted, pointing to the clock on the nightstand. I was almost ready to go. I only had to finish doing my makeup.

Marcus looked longingly at me with his dark-brown eyes. "Never too late for a kiss. Right, baby?"

"Right," I agreed, setting down my lipstick. I would never trade in a kiss from Marcus for anything, and I relaxed enough to let him embrace me. Marcus took full advantage of the situation. While he bit my bottom lip, he traced the mother-of-pearl buttons running down the front of my silk shirt, and then gently ran his fingertips over my breasts. My nipples grew hard instantly, and I had to force myself to stay focused on the time.

"We'll have fun tonight," I told him. "I promise. I'll be all yours then."

"Five minutes," he begged, taking my hand and placing it on the crotch of his jeans. "Just five minutes."

"I can't," I insisted. As I spoke, the front bell rang. "That's Carla. She's picking me up today."

"I know she is," Marcus said, confusing me because I didn't remember telling him. Usually, I meet Carla at her apartment. But I couldn't make sense of his words at that moment because Marcus had wrapped his hands in my long dark hair and pulled me to his chest in a tight bear hug. I felt his impressive morning hard-on through his faded jeans, and my resolve to be a good employee wavered dangerously until the doorbell rang again. I was going to have to change my panties before heading out to work. Marcus's kiss had made me all wet.

"I have to go." I sprinted down the hall to the door with Marcus trailing after me. I decided that I'd have Carla wait in the living room while I went back to the bedroom and chose a new thong. As I opened the front door, I heard Marcus laughing softly behind me.

"That's a snazzy look," Carla said. "Although I'm not sure it's appropriate for work. Even on casual Friday." She raised her mirrored shades to anchor her streaked blonde hair out of her eyes and kept smiling at me in the most disconcerting fashion. I didn't know what she was talking about. But then I felt the cool morning breeze against my naked skin and looked down.

"Marcus!" I shouted, blushing as I tried to cover myself up. While we'd been kissing in the bedroom, he'd unbuttoned my blouse. My shirt was open to mid-waist, revealing both my lacy white bra and my stomach. "Were you going to let me leave for work looking like this?"

"You look beautiful," Carla told me, taking a few steps forward and closing the door behind her. I turned to glance back at her, surprised at the husky tone of her voice. Was it my imagination or was she dressed rather sexily herself? She wore a pastel-pink dress that hugged her curves. Her long legs were bare, and she'd chosen to complete her outfit with tie-up rose-colored espadrille sandals. "Absolutely beautiful," she repeated.

"That's what I thought," Marcus agreed. Slowly, they moved around me, and I started to feel certain that something was going on that I didn't know about. When Marcus stood behind me and wrapped his arms around my waist while Carla came forward to kiss my parted lips, I knew that I was right. But that didn't stop me from pressing my lips to my pretty coworker's and giving in to the desire building within me. Again, I could feel Marcus's erection, but now he was pressing his rock-hard cock firmly against my ass. I was so wet that I thought I might melt entirely right there between the two of them. When Carla started to caress my breasts as she kissed me, I sighed loudly. Her touch was maddeningly light, her fingertips gently grazing my skin. I longed to have her touch me harder, to feel her hands cupping my breasts, squeezing them firmly as we continued to make out.

"We're going to be late," I stammered when we parted, as if it mattered. There I was, half-naked, kissing a coworker while my boyfriend happily participated, and I was babbling about work.

Carla quickly set me straight. "We're not going to work today," she said matter-of-factly as she set her sunglasses down on our living room end table.

"We're not?"

"No, you're not," Marcus repeated.

I looked at Marcus, who was regarding me with one of his sexy smirks. He had his hands all over me now, carefully undoing the rest of the buttons on my blouse before unsnapping my bra.

"Exactly what's going on?" I murmured dumbly, catching my bra in my hands and then cradling my arms in front of my naked breasts. I was dizzy with lust, as if I were in a dream. It wasn't a bad feeling at all, I realized to my surprise, and when Carla knelt in front of me and began unfastening the zipper on the side of my skirt, I didn't say a word. I simply watched her part the navy-blue fabric and slide the garment down over my hips. Her fingers on my thighs set my skin on fire, even through my stockings.

"You know that secret fantasy you confessed to me the other night?" Marcus asked, pulling my arms open and taking my shirt off me.

Of course, I knew, but my cheeks flamed up at the memory. First, we'd shared a half bottle of red wine, and then we'd shared X-rated fantasies. Luckily, ours meshed. He wanted to experience a ménage à trois with me and another girl, and I wanted to invite my beautiful friend Carla to join us in the bedroom. From the beginning, we'd always had a flirtatious relationship, but even as I whispered my desires, I knew I'd never have the nerve to turn my fantasy into reality. But apparently Marcus had.

"I called us in sick," Carla explained from her position at my feet. She looked up at me approvingly, stroking her fingertips along the lacy tops of my stockings. They were my sexiest pair, and I was secretly glad I'd chosen to wear them today. "I said that we'd been up late last night working on our project and we'd worn ourselves ragged. I promised to have it ready first thing Monday morning. Ms. Delacorte was very reasonable when I told her we'd be working through the weekend."

"You did all that without me knowing?" I asked, not really caring about her answer. She was on her knees with her face pressed to my panty-clad pussy, and her tongue had flicked out to touch my clit. I felt suddenly off balance, but Marcus was right behind me, supporting me as Carla licked my cunt through my panties. Her warm breath and wet tongue aroused me greatly, even through the fabric barrier, and I desperately wanted to feel her kissing my naked skin. Marcus must have sensed my unspoken desire, because he brought me over to our large red sofa and motioned for Carla to join us. In moments, I was spread out against the velvety pillows and Carla was nestled between my thighs, pulling my panties down. I gasped as she parted my nether lips with her fingers and then brought her mouth to my waiting pussy. I leaned my head back against the cushions and closed my eyes, but Marcus would have none of that.

"Look at me," he whispered, and I automatically obeyed his command, staring up at him as Carla continued to treat me to the most delicious pussy-licking I could imagine. Marcus caressed my heaving breasts as we stared into each other's eyes. It was the most amazing feeling to have Marcus touching me while my friend was lapping at my cunt. She parted my lips so wide that I felt an ache deep within myself, a hunger that made me crave everything she had to give. Then she brought her mouth directly to my clit, ringing it with her lips while her tongue expertly stroked it again and again. I squirmed and moaned, reveling in every sensation. Carla seemed to know exactly how to touch me. She teased me by running her tongue around my clit, not touching it directly, and then she rapped on it firmly and I spiraled with pleasure. It felt so good, but suddenly I wanted more.

"I want to taste you," I said, reaching my fingers down to touch her sun-streaked hair. "Please."

Carla was quick to oblige. She stood and shed her dress in a single motion, and I sucked in my breath when I saw that she was entirely naked under that pale-pink sheath. "I came prepared." She smiled, cocking her hip in a model's pose. She was cleanly shaved, her pussy totally bare. Her tanned skin gleamed in the morning sunlight. Just looking at her made me ravenous, and I was thrilled when she moved back to the sofa and climbed on top of me to form a sexy sixty-nine.

I had never tasted a woman's pussy before, but I didn't hesitate. I felt Marcus watching as I used my thumbs to spread her slick lips and then brought my tongue carefully to her clit. I worked softly at first until Carla said, "Harder, baby. Let me feel it."

That gave me the freedom to flutter my tongue firmly against her puffy clit. Her juices spread quickly to my lips and cheeks, and I savored the glossy sensation of being drenched in her erotic liquid. I paid attention to what she was doing between my own legs and worked to mirror her every motion. I drank from her, and then ran my tongue in circles around her clit. When I turned my head slightly, I saw Marcus sitting in the easy chair opposite us, his jeans spread open, his hand stroking his cock. He was transfixed, and I could tell he was loving every minute of this. My heart beat faster at the sight of him watching us. I realized we were putting on a show for him, even as we were reveling in our own enjoyment. I couldn't decide which concept was sexier, but then I had to stop thinking and focus my attention on the prize in front of me, licking and lapping as Carla worked to bring me to orgasm. I didn't sense it before it happened. All of a sudden, I was just coming, hard and furiously, bucking against her mouth. As I came, I continued to suck on her clit as if it were a piece of hard candy. My actions helped her reach her own climax, so that we came together, like one being. Carla reached her peak quietly, which surprised me. I thought she'd be a screamer, but instead, she was nearly silent, her body shaking with the power of her orgasm. For some reason this quiet crumbling made me even more aroused. I wanted to break her down, to make her scream next time. And I knew the next time would be soon.

We lay there, shuddering, for several moments, breathless and dazed, until finally I could speak again.

"Marcus," I said softly, "let's go to the bedroom. We need more space."

The three of us headed quickly down the hall. I was first, naked except for my garters and stockings. I had Carla's hand in mine and pulled her along after me. Marcus trailed behind us, and when I looked over my shoulder I saw that he was shedding his clothes on the journey. By the time we reached our room, he was only wearing his blue-and-white-striped boxers. Carla and I didn't say a word. We grabbed Marcus and pushed him backward onto the bed. Carla pulled his boxers off and threw them into a corner. I sensed from the expression on Marcus's face that he liked being stripped by another woman.

I climbed on one side of him, and she took the other. While I sucked his hard cock, she began to tickle his balls with the tip of her tongue. The two of us were pressing our breasts against him, touching him in similar ways, echoing each other's sexy actions.

Marcus moaned loudly and arched his back, and I took that as a sign to change positions with my girlfriend. Carla started to bob up and down on his cock while I bathed his balls in the warm, wet heat of my mouth.

"Oh, girls," he sighed, his whole body trembling. "Oh, my girls."

"He's ready," Carla murmured to me, and then she raised her blonde eyebrows, asking a silent question. I nodded and immediately she climbed astride his straining hard-on. Marcus's eyes held mine as Carla lowered herself onto his cock. I gazed at him as long as I could, but then I became too captivated by Carla's undulating body. I knelt at her side and licked her lovely nipples, first one, then the other. Then I pinched them both between my fingers and thumbs while Carla groaned and pumped harder up and down on Marcus's cock.

"You come here," he said, grabbing for me. Soon I was straddling his mouth while facing Carla. As we both rode him, we wrung every last drop of pleasure from his body. Marcus teased my ripe clit with his tongue and teeth, while Carla stroked her fingers along my ribs and up to my breasts. She and I leaned forward and kissed each other, and I thought I might lose all control. We made the perfect triangle as Marcus thrust his cock into her pussy and his tongue into mine. I was awash in erotic shivers, my whole body on fire, when Carla breathlessly said, "Switch!"

Moving from my front-row seat was heartbreaking. I had to pull my pulsing pussy away from Marcus's delicious mouth and tantalizing tongue, but when I saw his glistening cock so hard and ready for me, I couldn't wait to impale myself on it. I had him between my thighs in seconds, while Carla took over where I had left off, her pussy poised over Marcus's waiting mouth.

He started up again, and I felt the climax quickly building within me, making it hard for me to breathe. I was so turned on from watching my beautiful friend growing more aroused by the moment that I wanted to scream. Being filled to overflowing with Marcus's hard cock also felt divine.

"I'm going to—" I started to say.

"Don't you dare," Carla insisted. "We'll all come together. That's how it should be. You'll just have to wait until Marcus is ready."

"Are you?" I moaned. "Are you ready to come, Marcus?"

His reply was muffled against Carla's cunt, but I could tell he said, "Yes."

"Now?" I asked Carla. "Are you ready?" My voice bordered on desperation. I knew I couldn't hold back much longer. What if she said no? What if she told me to wait?

To my great relief, she said, "Yes. Now, sweetheart. Now!"

I ground my hips against Marcus and felt him explode inside me. Each thrust, each pump of his hips against mine, brought me higher.

"Come for me," I said, looking deep into Carla's eyes. "Let me hear it."

She matched my gaze, watching me fiercely as those amazing tremors began to rumble through my body. As if gaining strength from me, she parted her lips and let out the most musical moans. "Oh, sweetie," she whispered.

"Louder!"

"Oh!" she cried out, and the sound of her untamed voice made me come like a powerhouse. As those magical vibrations beat through my body, Carla leaned forward and kissed me and, joined like that, the three of us climaxed together.

For several moments, nobody spoke. Then Carla slid over to Marcus's side, and she ran her fingertips up and down her own body as she gazed at me. I pulled myself off Marcus and found a place on his other side, sandwiching him between us. The three of us huddled like that, warm and satisfied in the center of the bed. Then Carla looked at the clock.

"Think of all those people at their desks right now." She giggled.

"Or rushing in," Marcus said, "late for work." He tickled me, and I started to laugh, remembering how out of control I'd been earlier this morning, hurrying while he watched me. That whole time, he'd known that my rush was futile and that his secret plan would kick into effect at any moment.

"We have nothing else to do all day but fuck," Carla said, leaning over Marcus to kiss me firmly on the lips.

"But remember," Marcus said from below us, "you two are supposed to put in a lot of overtime this weekend."

"Oh yeah," Carla said, giggling uncontrollably again. This time I couldn't help but join her, and the three of us repeated the word together: "Overtime."

A Bold Invitation

KELLY MAYS

I recently moved from my small town to a large city and got a job as an administrative assistant at a software company. Initially, the office manager at my new company rubbed me the wrong way. Her name was Melissa, and in many aspects she was the exact opposite of me. She wore flamboyant clothes, with lots of short skirts and high heels. She kept her fingernails long and elaborately manicured. She was loud and brash, where I was quiet and reserved. While she was tall, with an olive complexion, dark eyes and long, silky dark hair, I am a petite, curly-haired redhead with bright-blue eyes, pale skin and a galaxy of freckles all over my body.

It wasn't too long, though, before Melissa and I actually became friends. Despite her brusque demeanor, she was a good-hearted person.

She took me under her wing and helped me learn my job duties quickly. Understanding that I was alone in a new city, she also sought to involve me in many social activities, which is how I met her boyfriend, Jeff. He was a good-looking, athletic fellow, with a cocky swagger that matched Melissa's boisterous personality.

Melissa and I often went out shopping on our lunch hour, and she would frequently talk about her sex life—and get a real kick out of raising my eyebrows. She mentioned that she and Jeff liked to watch porn movies and got a lot of sex tips from them. Her vivid descriptions left me speechless.

"The one thing we're dying to try is having another woman join us in bed," she told me one day while we were getting makeovers at a department store. "But I don't know who to invite."

At the time, I was too shocked by this revelation to even imagine that she was implying that she wanted me to join Jeff and her in bed. When I didn't respond immediately, she didn't say anything more about it. So, a few months rolled by and Melissa invited me over to her place for a barbecue. I assumed I was going to be one of many guests, but it turned out it was only the three of us. Jeff cooked up some steaks and poured us wine, and everyone was having a wonderful time. Then Melissa suggested we get into their outdoor hot tub, which was next to their deck.

"I didn't bring a swimsuit," I said naively, not yet sophisticated enough to pick up on their signals.

"You can use one of mine if you want," Melissa replied. "But we usually don't wear them."

My heart skipped a beat. I took a look around the backyard. It was secluded with high hedges. No one could see in. Jeff pulled off his shirt and then dropped his pants, while Melissa slipped out of her dress. Standing there in her bra and panties, she flashed me a big smile as if to say, "Well?"

I took a deep breath and decided to go for it. I kicked off my leather sandals and shyly turned away from them to unbutton my blouse. As it fell to the ground I realized I was becoming incredibly turned on and, it seemed, ready for anything. I shimmied out of my shorts and turned back around, wearing only my underwear.

Melissa was gloriously naked and beaming at me. I held my breath as I took in the sight of her magnificent body. My eyes traveled up her toned legs to her small firm breasts. I was surprised and pleased to see that she had a completely shaved pussy.

I tried not to stare at her naked sex too much and looked at Jeff, who was already in the bubbling water. I appreciatively noted his broad chest and large biceps. "Come on in!" he shouted. "The water's great!"

Melissa slipped into the steaming water. I fingered my bra strap, understanding that if I took it off I wasn't going to turn back. After the slightest hesitation, I unsnapped my bra, slipped off my panties and quickly slid into the warm water.

For a while nothing unusual happened. As we chatted, I caught Jeff eyeing me, but otherwise he made no move to touch me. Before long, though, I noticed something poking above the water between Jeff's legs. It was, of course, his cock, which was fully erect and quite large. Melissa noticed it, too, and reached over to grasp it.

My friend looked up at me with a searching glance. "We don't want to push you into anything," she said in a gentle voice. "You can leave, and we'll pretend it never even came up."

I paused and gave her an answer by sliding over and sitting

next to Jeff. I slowly reached out and touched the tip of his dick. He shuddered, and we all laughed. The game had begun.

Melissa's hand traveled up and down the length of Jeff's cock with measured strokes. He turned his head to me, and I gave him a peck on the lips. Then he leaned down and nuzzled my breasts, taking one of my hard nipples into his mouth. He sucked on it and I groaned, because it had been a while since I'd had the attention of a man. Instinctively, I put my hand between my legs and rubbed my pussy. Then I noticed I was right near one of the jets in the hot tub, and I shifted so that the pulsing water surged against my opening, making me shiver.

Jeff stood up, and I watched entranced as Melissa took his hard-on into her mouth. I played with his balls as she bobbed her head up and down on him. It soon became apparent the action was too much for him. Standing on shaky legs, he put his hand on Melissa's head and asked her to stop.

"I'm about ready to come," he panted.

"Why don't we take this inside?" she suggested, and we all stepped out of the water, wrapped ourselves in towels and scurried into their house. We made a beeline for their bedroom, and once there, we threw aside the damp towels and sprawled on their king-size bed.

Jeff was lying on his back, his erection pointing toward the ceiling. He and Melissa were engaged in a deep French kiss, so I decided to go for it and took his balls into my hand, caressing and fondling them. Then I teased them with my lips and tongue. Jeff stroked my hair while I sucked on his balls and stroked his cock. Eventually, I began tracing a line up the base of his shaft with my tongue, and then right on to the tip before enveloping him entirely.

I noticed out of the corner of my eye that Melissa was squatting above his face, her hairless cunt an inch from his mouth. Jeff shifted slightly so he could lick her pussy. She growled as he began to eat her, and I stopped to watch, feeling his dick pulse in my mouth.

After a while we switched positions. I was on my back, and Jeff knelt between my legs. He leaned down and nibbled softly on my labia and flicked his fingers against my clit. Melissa settled herself behind him, licking and playing with his balls as he moaned against my wet flesh.

This was all too much for me, and I felt an orgasm begin to sweep through my body. I pressed my thighs against Jeff's ears while he sucked on my clit and slid two fingers deep inside my pussy. My vaginal muscles clamped down on his fingers, and my climax washed over me like a summer storm.

Jeff got up on his knees, and Melissa, on all fours, resumed sucking his cock. After enjoying a few moments of her languorous tongue bath, Jeff grabbed hold of her long black hair and held her still as he fucked her mouth. Mesmerized, I played with my tits as he cried out and filled her mouth with his load.

Melissa slid up against me and gave me a kiss on the mouth. I was surprised by her sudden action—and by the strong taste of semen that lingered on her lips.

The three of us lay together in a euphoric afterglow, with Jeff in the middle. I was transfixed by the sight of his cock regaining its former glory, and even happier when he rolled over and slid it inside me. I wrapped both of my legs around his torso and hung on for the ride. His strokes were strong and deep, and I felt his balls slap against me. I don't know what Melissa was up to, because my eyes were closed and I could focus on nothing but how wonderfully I was being fucked.

A bit later we shifted positions so he could fuck me doggie-style, which is the way I like it best. Every one of his thrusts shook me to my core, and then, in a moment I will never forget, I opened my eyes and realized that Melissa's naked cunt was right in front of me.

She was on her back, her legs splayed wide, pulling on her nipples and smiling at me. This was certainly a bold invitation, and who was I to refuse? I stuck my tongue out and lightly licked her vulva. She tasted divine, and in seconds my face was buried in her sex as my fingers worked their way inside her slick tunnel. Jeff was still fucking me hard, so it was difficult to keep my mouth from coming off her pussy, but I did my best. Melissa certainly wasn't complaining—rather she was cooing and moaning with each swipe of my tongue.

Jeff sped up his thrusts as he approached his orgasm. "I want to feel you come inside me," I screamed, never having uttered such words before. He promptly granted my request, and the sensation of his semen filling my pussy was electrifying. Once he pulled out, Melissa had me lie back so she could eat her man's load out of my cunt. The whole thing was so outrageous—and I loved every minute of it.

Before the night was over, I looked on happily as Jeff fucked his girlfriend, and I got a chance to revisit Melissa's pussy, where I licked her until she climaxed. I gladly accepted their offer to stay over, and we all played in the shower before turning in for the night.

That summer I hooked up with Jeff and Melissa a few more times. Being with them triggered something in my brain. It was as if the floodgates were opened, and I became more aware of my sexuality than ever before. At the end of the summer, I wanted to do something even more adventurous, so I booked a trip to a singles resort in the Caribbean. I figured it would be much easier for me to let my hair down when I was away from home, in a place where nobody knew me.

Melissa drove me to the airport and wished me luck with a kiss. I was so nervous when I arrived at the resort, looking at all the men and wondering if I would have sex with them. I attracted quite a few stares of my own, and the strangers' attention gave me quite a rush.

The first night there I met a pair of guys from Boston. As we sat around the pool and drank cocktails under a starry sky, I immediately connected with them. We told stories and laughed quite a bit. Tim was tall and shy. He must have been at least six-four, with brooding good looks and a reserved demeanor. His friend, Brendan, was shorter and scrappier, with a gift for telling jokes. I thought both were attractive, and I could tell they each liked me. My only problem was that I couldn't figure out which one I liked better, but then it suddenly occurred to me that I didn't have to choose.

I excused myself and went to the ladies' room to splash cold water on my face and fully decide whether I wanted to go through with this. Of course, I didn't know if the guys would go for it. When I came back to our table I had to laugh. Brendan and Tim were playing rock-paper-scissors. It appeared that Tim had won, because Brendan's head mockingly fell as if in crushing defeat.

"Lose something?" I asked Brendan cheerily.

"Uh, yeah," Brendan said. "Let me leave you two alone."

"There's no need," I said, sitting down beside him and running my hand along his arm. "There's enough of me for both of you to share."

The guys looked at me in amazement. Then their faces indicated an unspoken question, which I answered by smiling and nodding my head. I stood and told them my room number.

"Meet me there in five minutes," I said. "Both of you."

When I got to my room I was almost hyperventilating with excitement. After six or seven minutes of impatient waiting I started to lose hope. After all, most men aren't accustomed to sharing a woman sexually. But just when I was ready to give up and take my vibrator to bed with me, I heard a knock on the door. I opened it, and Tim was standing there. *Oh well*, I thought, *Brendan must not have been up for it.* I welcomed Tim in, but as I was about to shut the door, Brendan came running up the hallway.

I was so overjoyed to see him that I laughed and took him in my arms, kissing him with a questing tongue. Brendan was such a good kisser that I nearly swooned with excitement. He kept me upright and danced me over to the bed. We fell onto it, and I began unbuttoning his shirt. I looked up and saw that Tim had sat down in a chair. "Come on, don't be shy," I told him. He stood up and hesitantly approached the bed. By now Brendan's busy hands had pushed my tank top above my tits and were fondling them excitedly. When Tim was standing next to the bed, I reached over and caressed his package through his shorts. He groaned and quickly grew fully erect.

As Brendan suckled my nipples, I pulled Tim's shorts and underwear down, releasing his long, fine-looking cock. I stroked it, enjoying how it throbbed in my grip. Brendan had now pulled my skirt off and was licking my pussy through my panties. When I bucked toward him impatiently, he pushed aside the fabric and wiggled his tongue against my moistening slit.

I lifted my legs to allow him easier access. With that repositioning, I pulled Tim onto his knees beside me on the bed. He put a couple of pillows beneath my head and then slowly fed me his cock. At first I licked it like a lollipop, but when its surface was slick with my saliva, I took his entire length into my mouth. Tim moaned and humped his hips toward my face.

Meanwhile, Brendan was burrowing his stiff tongue deep into my vagina while his fingers rimmed my asshole. I wanted more than his gentle teasing, and in between panting breaths I said, "Put your finger in my ass."

He grinned, licked his index and middle fingers and worked them into my back hole. As I would later learn, it was typical for Brendan to give me two fingers when I asked for one. The feeling was deliriously wonderful: Brendan's tongue dancing against my clit, his fingers thrusting in and out of my asshole, and Tim's cock buried in my mouth up to his balls. I was in a sexual frenzy, and it was only beginning.

Brendan quickly brought me to orgasm, and I nearly crushed the poor man's skull with my thighs. When I released him, he stood and removed his clothes. I shifted around on the bed until I was on all fours and then sucked his thick cock. Tim was behind me, and he licked my pussy a bit before I felt his cock spreading my labia. He slipped into my wetness easily and began fucking me in earnest.

How can I describe how wonderful it was to be filled from both ends? My only regret is that there was no one there to film it. Many times since then I have masturbated, imagining what we must have looked like, and every time I do, I come like crazy.

In just a few minutes, Brendan signaled that he was going to come. He was probably used to girls who backed off, but I was just the opposite. I grabbed his ass and squeezed it hard, indicating that he shouldn't dare pull away. Seconds later, his cock pulsed and his come filled my mouth. I swallowed every drop, savoring his creamy taste.

Brendan was completely spent and lay back to watch Tim fuck

me. He put my feet on his shoulders, making me feel every inch of his dick. My head hung off the edge of the bed, so I looked through the glass doors to the terrace upside-down. I was so dizzy with pleasure that when I came I didn't know which way was up. Tim came a moment later, and I felt deliciously dirty knowing that I had two loads of semen inside me.

Tim wandered off to the bathroom, and by this time, Brendan and I were both ready for more action. "I want you to fuck me in the ass," I blurted out and his face lit up.

"That's my favorite," he gushed, and I believed him. I told him I had some lube in the drawer of the bedside table. He slathered his cock and lubed up my asshole. Lying on my side, I lifted my leg and he maneuvered his revived cock into my anus. He moved slowly, and I closed my eyes to savor the sensations. When I felt his balls press up against my cheeks, I was overwhelmed by a profound sense of fulfilling pleasure.

As Brendan fucked my ass, Tim came out of the bathroom, his cock swinging in front of him. The sight of our coupling stopped him in his tracks and his dick began to grow. I recalled the double-penetration scenes I had seen in many porn movies, and though I never imagined I could do it, I was now going to try.

I had Brendan lie on his back while I sat on his cock, facing away from him in a reverse-cowgirl position until he was firmly up my ass. Then I lay back against his chest, putting my feet on his thighs. My dripping pussy was now fully open and available for Tim.

"Come fuck me, Tim," I panted, as Brendan writhed beneath me, grinding his cock in my rear end. Tim played with his own rock-hard erection and got in between Brendan's spread legs. He crawled on top of me, and, below me, I felt Brendan take a deep breath. Tim guided his erection into my pussy, and I groaned. Brendan surged upward, and his cock pressed deeper inside my ass. The guys quickly developed a rhythm, and before long one dick was pulling out as another was pushed in. Meanwhile, I was so lost in ecstasy that I would have been hard-pressed to remember my name.

After a few minutes, we sought a more comfortable position. Tim lay on his back, and I squatted above him, face-to-face, and lowered my pussy onto his cock. Then Brendan approached me from behind and reentered my asshole. This position allowed me to fuck both of their hard cocks, and I was soon trembling uncontrollably in orgasm. The guys gently pulled out of me and lay me on the bed between them, stroking my naked body and murmuring sweetly in my ears.

Sometime later I came back to earth. When I realized both Brendan and Tim were still hard, since they hadn't come during my double-penetration, I got another devilish idea. "Both of you come for me," I told them matter-of-factly. "I want to watch you shoot off."

They eyed each other and shrugged. "Why not?" they both seemed to say with body language. With Brendan kneeling on my left and Tim on my right, they both began to stroke their ready-to-burst erections.

I lay back and drank in the vision of these two fine men stroking their cocks just for me. I reached up and fondled a set of balls with each hand. That was too much for Brendan, who squirted his seed all over my tits. Tim followed within a minute, splattering his come on the bed beside me.

Afterward, we all lay where we were for quite a while. Eventually, the guys stood up, got dressed, kissed me good night and left. I awoke hours later in exactly the same spot, buck naked and still sticky with come. It had truly been the best night of my life.

I had several more lusty adventures during that memorable trip, with both Brendan and Tim separately and a few other sexy men. My night with the two boys from Boston, however, was undoubtedly my favorite one, and the guys have promised to visit me—together—sometime soon. I can hardly wait.

Summer Loving

DIRK GOLDMAN

Summer and I flopped down on a park bench after a brisk jog along the waterfront. It was the day after Thanksgiving, a good day for people-watching.

I glanced at my girlfriend and smiled. Even after our lengthy jog, Summer looked great. It didn't matter that her face was flushed and sweaty, or that her long, thick black hair was in disarray, or even that her luscious figure was clad in gray sweatpants and an old T-shirt. She's tall and dark-eyed, with a permanent San Diego tan and a fit, curvy body that makes people stare, no matter what she's wearing.

"Hey, Dirk." Summer directed my attention to a jogger who was coming up the path. "She's pretty." As the young woman got closer, Summer amended her assessment. "Actually, she's *hot*."

To my surprise, I recognized the jogger. It was Emily, my girl-friend before Summer. I hadn't seen her in more than a year but it was easy to remember the intense physical connection that had dominated our relationship. Sex with Emily had been vigorous and frequent. It was fun while it lasted, but eventually Emily wanted to spread her wings and see the world, while I needed to stay in San Diego and finish graduate school. Our split was amicable; we parted as friends. Now here she was again, looking better than ever—green eyes, small nose, creamy skin, blonde hair bouncing as she jogged toward us. She was dressed to show off her toned body.

I glanced at Summer and thought, *This is going to be awkward.* But then I reminded myself that Summer is a very confident woman and hardly the jealous type; in fact she's as easygoing as anyone I've ever met. I probably had even less to worry about with Emily—wild, insatiable Emily, with whom I'd once had a threesome involving another woman. It had been Em's idea, and it had gone over spectacularly.

When my old lover caught sight of me, her eyes flew open wide. "Dirk! Oh my gosh!" she exclaimed.

Summer shot me a sidelong glance and whispered, "Don't tell me—an old flame?"

"Afraid so." I smiled and waved, and then there was no more time for hushed remarks, because Emily was hugging me and laughing with delight. After a moment I extricated myself and introduced her to Summer, who was watching with a bemused expression. Upon hearing Emily's name, her eyebrows went up. "It's nice to be able to put a face with a name," she said.

"Oh, has Dirk told you about me?" Emily asked.

"A little." I had mentioned the threesome. Summer had been fascinated, demanding details. Meeting her gaze now, I could see that her interest was seriously piqued. Emily seemed equally intrigued by Summer as the two women took stock of each other. Summer is by nature a warm, charismatic person with a sunny disposition, truly deserving of her name. Everyone who meets her likes her immediately, and I could see it was the same with Emily.

"You have me at a disadvantage," Emily said, "because I know nothing about you." Her tone was playful, her smile suddenly coy.

"Well," my impetuous girlfriend replied, "why don't you come up to our place and have a drink with us?"

This caught me off guard. Emily seemed surprised, too, but also glad. My girlfriend looked at me, searching my face for a reaction. I found myself more than happy to go along. There was something exciting brewing, I could tell.

"Sure, that's a great idea," I said. "It would be good to catch up, Em."

Emily looked at the ground and kicked a stone. When she raised her head again, her grin was even more mischievous. "Okay, why not?" she said.

We gave her our address and agreed to expect her around five that afternoon. We talked a while longer, reluctant to cut off whatever it was that was building among us. Summer and Emily chatted effortlessly, becoming fast friends before my eyes. "Well, see you at five," Emily said at last, and she jogged off.

Back in the apartment, Summer was especially frisky as we showered and rubbed soapy lather all over each other. I cupped my hands over her breasts and lightly tweaked the coral-hued nipples until they were as stiff as my cock. She felt my erection against her belly and curled her hand around it. One thing would certainly have led to another if the doorbell hadn't sounded just then.

I threw a towel around my waist and went to the door. Emily looked great in a fitted shirt and leather skirt. My cock was still hard from the shower play with Summer; it lifted my towel like a tent pole. Naturally, Emily's gaze settled there. Her expression immediately turned devilish. It was a look I'd seen often when we had been together, a look that often led to her most debauched behavior.

"Nice, Dirk," she said, with a smirk.

"Sorry, we lost track of time."

"Don't be sorry." The smirk deepened. She was so damn sexy.

"Come on in," I said, stepping aside. "I'll be right back. Make yourself comfortable. Here's Summer." She had just come into the room, barefoot and wearing jeans and a red T-shirt. Her wet hair was combed back. She smiled at Emily. I went to get dressed, leaving the two of them alone.

A short while later I rejoined them in the living room. They were sitting on the couch with margaritas in hand, whispering to each other like schoolgirls with a secret.

"I sense a conspiracy," I said.

Emily filled a glass from the pitcher on the coffee table and handed it to me. "Your girlfriend has an idea."

"Oh?"

Summer grinned. "She's been telling me about your threesome." It was impossible not to see the desire in her face. My cock stirred in my pants.

"I've already told you all about that," I said.

"It's worth hearing twice." Summer turned fully to me; her eyes flashed with outright lust. "Let's do it. The three of us."

My manhood unfurled the rest of the way and strained against the inside of my zipper. I got up from my easy chair and approached my companions. Emily leaned close to Summer, took her chin in hand and kissed her full on the lips. Summer didn't hesitate at all; she kissed Emily back with a vehemence that took my breath away. At the same time, Summer's fingers found the fly of my jeans and yanked the zipper down. I finished the job for her, unsnapping the button and pulling my jeans and boxer shorts down to my knees. My cock leaped into her hand. Summer kept making out with Emily while she ran her hand up and down my dick. Emily reached out, too, and fondled my heavy balls. The sight of their sapphic lip-lock and the touch of their hands all over my pleasure zone had my pulse racing.

Summer turned toward me and lowered her crimson lips over my penis. Emily ran her hands over Summer's body while she watched my girlfriend suck me. My heart pounded as Summer slid her lips down my pole as far as she could go. After a while, she leaned back and offered my dick to Emily, who greedily picked up where Summer had left off. Her technique was novel and yet familiar to me as she bobbed back and forth, stirring memories of the countless times she'd gone down on me in the past. Summer kissed and nibbled the back of Emily's neck while keeping an eye on my cock. When Emily yielded to her, Summer sealed her lips once more around my twitching rod. She slurped with such gusto that I felt a tingle at the base of my cock, signaling my impending release. Summer was practically syphoning the cream right out of my balls.

Recognizing that she'd taken me past the point of no return, Summer cried, "Come on, baby, squirt it!" As she pumped her hand up and down my pulsing shaft, Emily reached between my legs and grabbed my ass. She even slipped a finger into my crack. Almost immediately my cock began spouting milky ribbons of semen with a force that took all three of us by surprise. The first blast ended up in Summer's hair; the second lewdly festooned Emily's chin. After that the girls got matters under control and, taking turns at my crown, they swallowed the rest of my load.

I stumbled around to the easy chair and sat down for a minute. On the couch, Emily lifted Summer's shirt and reached inside to stroke her breasts. Anxious to help her, Summer pulled the shirt over her head. Then she helped Emily do the same. I was intrigued to see that neither of them wore a bra this afternoon, but then, neither Summer nor Emily really needed one. When they leaned toward each other for another scintillating kiss, Emily's firm, taut breasts pressed into Summer's slightly larger ones, and their stiff nipples rubbed together, eliciting murmurs of delight from both girls. Emily's hands were all over Summer's chest, stroking, tracing, learning the soft contours. Summer lowered her head and closed her lips over Emily's pink nubs to suck one, then the other. Emily's eyes closed, and she arched her back, feeding her flesh to the other woman's mouth.

While they were indisposed, I took my pants all the way off and my shirt, too. Then I went to the couch, knelt down and unbuttoned Summer's pants. It would have taken me a while to get them off her, considering how close fitting they were, but Summer disengaged herself from Emily and helped me. Her cotton thong went next, leaving her completely, dazzlingly nude. Emily stripped bare, too, while her gaze roamed over Summer's ripe body. The erotic flames in their eyes spoke volumes.

Emily lay back on the couch with insouciance, letting her legs splay open. When we had been together, Emily had always kept her vulva completely hair-free. It was just the same now; she was smooth and bald down there. Summer, on the other hand, keeps a narrow landing strip of curly black hair to adorn her pubic zone. Comparing them now, I couldn't decide which style I liked better—and then I almost laughed in amazement at having the opportunity to compare them side by side in the first place.

"Come here, Summer," Emily said, her voice sultry. "I want so badly for you to taste me."

Like a cat on the prowl, Summer crawled toward Emily on her hands and knees. Trembling with excitement, she lowered her shoulders and pressed her face into the *V* of Emily's crotch. I watched, mesmerized, as Emily pushed her cunt against my girlfriend's mouth. "Oh god, that's good," she murmured. Her hands flew to her breasts; her fingers pinched and pulled her nipples. Summer's face was partly hidden by Emily's flexing thighs, but I could see her head moving up, down and side to side as she worked her tongue vigorously in Emily's succulent folds. Summer's breasts were flattened against the couch and her ass was up in the air behind her, looking incredibly inviting. It was time for me to get back into the action.

My rejuvenated cock was leaking precome as I knelt on the couch behind Summer. She looked so smutty like that, with her ass up and her face down in another woman's pussy, that for a moment I could only stop and stare. My lust soon got the better of me, though. Quick as a flash I slotted my dick between Summer's swollen cunt lips and rocked forward. She cried out with delight and lifted her head to look back at me with a sloppy grin. Then she turned her attention back to Emily's clit while I buried my manhood to the hilt in her juicy hole. My rhythm was slow at first, almost indolent, which made Summer wiggle her hips impatiently at me. Soon, however, I let the fever take hold and began fucking her with the amped-up energy she craved. Summer undulated wildly between Em and me, as waves of passion rolled through her slinky frame. I knew it wouldn't take much more to make her climax.

Hooking my hands around Summer's hips, I pumped ferociously into the confines of her cunt. Each time I plunged home, she lurched toward Emily's sex. I imagined her lips mashing against Emily's plump clit and her tongue forging deeply into Emily's hole. Emily grabbed fistfuls of Summer's hair and bucked her hips off the couch to meet Summer's tongue. A moment later Emily went mad, her whole body twisting and writhing in ecstasy. Summer kept right on licking with gusto, as if Emily's sex juices were the sweetest nectar she had ever tasted. I kept up my end, too, pounding away at Summer with abandon. I could hardly believe I was in a threeway involving my former and present girlfriends.

Emily, who was still catching her breath, wriggled off the couch and crawled back to me so she could see the finale up close. She stroked my ass with one hand and Summer's back with the other. Summer rocked against me freely now, a sex machine hell-bent on sending us both over the edge. It didn't take long. "Oh fuck—I'm coming!" she yelled. Her hands gripped the leather seat cushion with white-knuckled intensity.

"Here it comes," I rasped, as my balls prepared to empty themselves of all they had left.

"Come on her back. I want to see!" Emily cried. I pulled out of Summer just in time to shoot off all over her back and butt. Emily rubbed the sticky stuff into Summer's skin and then, with a lewd grin at both Summer and me, she licked her fingers clean.

We were all pretty wiped out after that, but Emily made no move to leave our place. I was glad, and so was Summer, who blurted, "Stay for dinner, will you? Oh hell, just stay the night!"

Emily agreed. We all showered, and then we enjoyed some Thanksgiving leftovers. It was late by the time we finished cleaning up. Emily joined us in our bed, which was roomy enough for three. The girls sandwiched me, arranging themselves on either side. I'd never had such a sensual send-off to sleep as I did that night.

Sometime later, in the wee hours of the morning, I woke up when I felt the bed moving. I opened my eyes but the room was so dark, I could hardly see anything. Quiet, mewling sounds of feminine pleasure brought me fully awake. As my eyes adjusted to the darkness, I saw that Emily was crouched between Summer's knees and her head was deep between Summer's thighs. Summer moaned and raked her hands through Emily's blonde locks. I looked at Summer's face and saw the raw passion there, the unabashed lust that turned her eyes bright and feverish. She stared back at me, looking so completely turned on that my penis instantly hardened. My girlfriend was getting oral from my ex and loving it.

Emily must have zeroed in on her clit just then, because Summer gasped and raised herself up on her elbows. She grabbed her quivering breasts and squeezed them together. Emily tongued her more ardently still, making Summer thrash about. The mattress springs sent up an outcry. "Ah, yes!" Summer exclaimed, going tense all over. She let out a long, whispery sigh of satisfaction that belied the true depth of her orgasm.

"I'm glad you're awake," Emily said at last, looking at me with a concupiscent smile. She crawled over and pulled the sheets down to my knees, exposing my rock-hard dick. "I've never forgotten what a lovely cock you have, Dirk," she went on. "So heavy and thick…" She ran a finger down the underside of my shaft, then back up to trace circles around the meaty crown. Without another word, she lowered her mouth over my glans. Her lips were still sloppy with Summer's juices.

Summer joined in at once, kissing and licking all over my staff's lower half, and my balls, too. She stopped only long enough to say, "We need you to fuck us, honey. Both of us, right now."

"That's right," Emily intoned with quiet urgency. "Do us both. Hard." Even as she said it she was already climbing aboard, demonstrating as she did so the physical agility I'd always admired about her. She settled her toned, lithe body over me and screwed herself down on my shaft with a moan of contentment. I remembered that silky grasp so well. Emily peered down to watch my cock disappear inside her, just as she always used to. Then she sat up straight and got busy lifting and lowering herself on my dick like she might never get another chance. Her stomach was tight and flat; I could see the vague outlines of her abdominal muscles as she powered herself like a piston atop my prick.

Meanwhile, Summer squatted over my face and lowered her slit onto my lips. Her scent filled my nose and her taste filled my mouth as I snaked my tongue into her soft folds. Working two fingers into the tight space between Summer's vulva and my mouth, I spread her nether lips open to better expose her dripping pink recesses. Her plump clit was ripe for the taking, so I sealed my lips to it and sucked in the way I knew she liked. Summer yelped with joy and mashed her cunt against my face. She was soon close to the edge, and when I reached up to press my wet thumb against her anus, she came hard, grinding her sex against my mouth.

Emily's passionate growls were growing louder, too. Her boundless sexual energy was on full display as she rose and fell on my cock like a woman bewitched. Her ass smacked down against my thighs faster and harder with every passing second, until finally I felt the primal spasm of her cunt and a corresponding gush of wetness. My dick was twitching and nearly ready to explode, but Emily rolled off me when her climax ebbed and lay on her back beside me. I knew from experience that she was hardly sated, just as I knew that Summer wanted more, too. As I watched, Summer climbed off me and crawled on top of Emily to form a sixty-nine. I knelt behind Summer and planted my prick in her sloppy cunt. Emily's face was between Summer's thighs, just below my balls. She stuck out her tongue and lapped at Summer's clit while I rocked my shaft in and out of Summer's hole. Desperate cries of passion rent the air again as our orgy of lust intensified. I felt a climax coming like an onrushing locomotive.

"Finish in my ass!" Summer yelled, lifting her head from Emily's crotch to look back at me. I imagined Emily's surprise upon hearing her plea, but I merely grinned and took it in stride. Summer often likes me to come in her backside. When I slid out of her pussy, I quickly grabbed some lube from the nightstand and slickened my shaft. Emily then reached up, grabbed my cock and held it to Summer's smallest hole. I pushed forward into my girl's amazing ass and didn't stop until I was completely buried between her cheeks. Emily went back to slurping and licking on Summer's pussy from below while I sawed away at my girlfriend's firm, round rump from behind. Summer reached an impressive climax in short order, bucking at me and babbling incoherently as her juices ran down onto Emily's tongue.

I couldn't hold off a second longer. Squeezing Summer's supple asscheeks in my hands, I slammed into her back door once more and released torrents of come into her steamy depths. Emily, her tongue still twirling in Summer's cunt, watched the whole thing from below, at point-blank range.

Exhausted, I fell back onto the bed. My companions crawled up on either side of me. We pulled the covers up and were soon asleep. When I opened my eyes again, late-morning sun streamed through the windows. Summer lay curled up at my side, sleeping contentedly, but Emily was gone. Her note on the nightstand read simply: *Until next time.*